MW00989991

THE
RELUCTANT
SHERIFF

Also by Chris Offutt

THE RELUCTANT SHERIFF

A MICK HARDIN NOVEL

CHRIS OFFUTT

Grove Press
New York

Excerpt from *The Ghosts of Belfast* by Stuart Neville, copyright © 2009 by
Stuart Neville. Used by permission of Soho Press, Inc. All rights reserved.

Published simultaneously in Canada
Printed in the United States of America

First Grove Atlantic US hardcover edition: March 2025

This book was set in 12-pt. Bembo
by Alpha Design & Composition of Pittsfield, NH.

Library of Congress Cataloging-in-Publication data is available for this title.

ISBN 978-0-8021-6403-2
eISBN 978-0-8021-6404-9

Grove Press
an imprint of Grove Atlantic
154 West 14th Street
New York, NY 10011

Distributed by Publishers Group West

groveatlantic.com

25 26 27 28   10 9 8 7 6 5 4 3 2 1

For Cade Smith
who never gave up

You can't choose where you belong, and where you don't.
But what if the place you don't belong
is the only place you have left?

—Stuart Neville

Chapter One

The employment application had a section about alcohol consumption and Harley Bolin lied that he never drank. Sometimes in the evening he had a glass of wine with his wife. She liked it with ice and he didn't mind it that way, but in the hills of eastern Kentucky, most men drank bourbon or beer. He didn't want word getting out that he went for sweet white wine from a far-fetched place like California.

Getting a job driving a truck that delivered liquor to bars was worth the lie. If he got caught, he could always say he didn't drink at the time he applied. He told the truth on everything else—graduated high school, three semesters at Rocksalt Community College, no criminal record, and a clean driving history. The company hired him. He was always on time and never missed work, which resulted in two raises his first year. The hours of jouncing in the high cab behind the wheel were offset by unloading cases of liquor and beer. It was a sweat-and-rest job, traveling five days a week in three counties.

Harley usually worked alone but this week he was breaking in a new guy, Ronnie something or other. The kid had just turned twenty-two, legally old enough to deliver, and talked nonstop the first half hour. Harley nodded and grunted in the hope that training Ronnie was a step toward promotion, a bigger territory, maybe even boss of the tri-county area. As Ronnie jabbered, Harley slowly increased the radio's volume until the kid got tired of yelling and slumped against the door, staring out the window.

One good thing about Ronnie, he wasn't afraid of work. At the warehouse he'd insisted on loading more than his share of boxes and took on the tricky task of shoving the metal ramp into its slot in the back of the truck. Harley was grateful. Last year a driver lost two fingers doing it and got fired. Harley's wife was pregnant with their second kid and he wanted to keep his fingers and his job.

The day's first stop was a Rocksalt liquor store housed in an old train station. The procedure was simple with friendly workers, quick paperwork, and plenty of room to maneuver the truck. Afterward, Harley headed out of town and cut the radio.

"Next is a bar," he said to Ronnie. "Bars ain't as easy as a store. Not a one has a loading dock. We got to wheel the boxes in on a hand truck."

"No probs," Ronnie said. "I did that at the IGA. If you think liquor is tough, wait till you're hauling a hundred pounds of hamburger frozen so cold it'll burn your hands. One time—"

"That's a lot of meat."

"Darn sure is. They were stocking up for Fourth of July. Wieners are the worst. They don't stack good. Don't worry, I can push any hand truck you got."

"You'll have to go slow," Harley said. "It has a gravel lot."

"What kind of gravel? Creek rock? Limestone? Crusher run?"

Harley turned the radio up and switched to a pre-eighties country station. He slowed to make a wide turn at a T-intersection, then kept the speed down for the half-mile drive to Ajax Bar and Grill. The tavern wasn't open yet but the owner was always inside waiting for delivery. Harley steered to the far edge of the lot, then put the truck in reverse.

Ronnie opened his door and jumped out.

"I'll guide you in," Ronnie said.

Harley ignored him. He was adept at backing up the truck and knew the precise place to stop so the metal ramp would end at the front door. He was intent on the side mirror when Ronnie started shouting and banging furiously on the side of the truck. Harley stopped abruptly, annoyed by the kid. He turned down the radio as Ronnie opened the door, his face pale.

"There's a man laying dead out here."

Chapter Two

Mick Hardin drove the official county vehicle along a narrow blacktop road that bisected the hills. He was filling in as sheriff while his sister recuperated from a gunshot wound sustained in the line of duty. This was Linda's official vehicle, and a Bigfoot air freshener swayed from the rearview mirror. It was a three-quarter profile view of Bigfoot in mid-stride, looking over his huge, hairy shoulder. The cardboard smelled of pine, or what the manufacturer thought pine trees smelled like, which wasn't the scent of any tree Mick knew. Earlier he'd given it an experimental sniff in case there was something lurking beneath the chemical tang, maybe ancient dirt or decaying moss. Nope, just fake pine like cheap bathroom cleaner.

During her recovery, Linda was temporarily living under the roof of Shifty Kissick while Mick stayed in his sister's house. Everything in his life was provisional, including his role as sheriff. He thought it was a kind of metaphor for the hills of eastern Kentucky, a temporariness that never changed. Only nature itself was consistent—relentless, beautiful, benevolent, and cruel.

He turned onto the long dirt driveway to the house of a woman who'd called the station three times. The SUV bounced through a mudhole, causing Bigfoot to hop against the windshield and bend a flimsy arm. It occurred to Mick that no one had ever found the giant bones of Bigfoot. The absence of a skeleton kept the legend alive. Or maybe they lived forever. It was a conversation for Johnny Boy, the former deputy, but he was on temporary leave, whereabouts unknown to everyone except Mick.

The driveway ended at a yard with an old Pontiac on the grass. Mick parked behind it, honked his horn, and got out. The one-story house gave the impression of being close to the ground due to the low slope of the roof that extended above the porch. The screen door opened and a woman in her late forties stepped outside smoking a cigarette. A midsize dog shot from the house, leaped the three steps, and bounded across the yard. Its tail wagged with such vigor that its hips moved as if dancing. Mick shifted his body to look at the dog peripherally and reduce his own threat.

"Conway!" the woman said.

The dog stopped moving.

"He's friendly," she said.

"I can see that," Mick said. "I'm Sheriff Hardin. Are you Mrs. Morris? Molly Morris?"

"Yes, I am. I called y'all three times."

"I understand, ma'am. We're short-staffed right now and got behind. How can I help you?"

"Around back," she said. "Loretta is up to no good. I don't hardly know where to start or how to say it."

"Let's start with Loretta. Who is she?"

"My daughter-in-law. Soon to be ex."

Mick nodded.

"Loretta what?" he said.

"Loretta Cargill. Kept her own name. That's how little she thinks of our family."

"A lot of women do that these days," Mick said. "Might not be personal."

"Are you a married man?"

"Divorced."

"Did she take your name?"

"Yes, she did. It was twenty years ago."

"Then how do you know what you're talking about with these young Jezebels and how they think?"

"I don't reckon I do," Mick said.

She tipped her head and gave it a quick nod, then took a long drag off her cigarette. She blew the smoke hard and fast as if making a point. Its funnel dissipated in a breeze. At the end of the porch, a robin poked its head from a forsythia bush to look at the humans.

"Your son," Mick said, "the one married to Loretta. Does he live here?"

"Well. Yes and no."

"It would help if you were a little more specific, Mrs. Morris."

"Ronnie and Loretta live around back but I ain't seen him in a few days. I'd just as soon Loretta left."

"Around back?"

"Yes, they made a damn yurt."

"A yurt."

"That's what they call it. Some kind of thing made out of sticks. It's a mess is what it is. Like a hideout little kids built in the woods. One hard wind and it's gone. I been praying for a big storm."

"Okay," Mick said. "Why did you call?"

"At first I thought Ronnie had a lot of new friends, but he's gone and there's men still coming around. My opinion, she's doing floozy business."

Mick nodded and looked at the forsythia bush. The robin had ducked back inside and Mick felt a jolt of envy for the ease with which it could avoid difficulties. Maybe the bird should be sheriff, or Mick should have been a bird.

He walked around the house to a long backyard snugged tight to the ubiquitous hillside. A pair of bee boxes stood near a patch of honeysuckle beside a heavy-duty push lawnmower suited to rough terrain. A mowed path led to a homemade shelter situated within the shade of a sugar maple. He'd seen yurts, a kind of round tent with a sturdy door, while serving in Afghanistan. This one had the traditional shape but it was covered by a shimmering blue tarp staked to the ground. The entrance was an old bear hide, the fur scraped off in sections, exposing the stiff yellow skin.

In front of the yurt was a small firepit built of stacked rock topped by a grate. Four lawn chairs surrounded it. A creek ran along the base of the hill below a damp cliff that was dripping water. Red and green moss glittered on the stone. Like most of eastern Kentucky, it resembled a park that families visited on vacation in other states. Here, the people just lived.

Mick went back to the front, faced the bear hide, and spoke.

"Hidy," he said. "Anybody in there?"

The bear hide rustled, then was shoved aside from within. Out stepped a woman in her twenties, moving with an elegance that surprised Mick, considering the situation. She looked him straight on with frank intelligence in her clear eyes. She glanced at the sheriff's badge and holstered Beretta, then back to his face. He nodded and stepped back.

"Loretta Cargill?" he said.

"That's me. Do you want to come in?"

"No, thank you. I'm all right out here."

"Is Ronnie hurt?"

"Not as far as I know," he said. "I'm not here about him."

"His mom okay?"

"I just talked to her and she's fine. Reason I'm here, she called three times."

Loretta walked to a lawn chair and sat. Mick took another chair and they stared across the dead fire at each other. A fly landed on the cooking grate, then another. The scent of honeysuckle drifted and Mick took a big inhale.

"One of my favorite smells," he said.

"It's a good pollinator. The butterflies need all the help they can get these days. Reckon we all do."

"Mrs. Morris thinks you're running some kind of business back here. Is that the case?"

"Sort of, yeah. People stop by. If they're in a hurry, I give them a pull."

"A pull."

"Yes. Sometimes they give me things. That bear hide. The lawn mower. It's self-propelled but the drivetrain quit working and the woman didn't want it. Heavy as heck but free's free, you know. Her two boys dropped it off. I gave them a free pull."

"A free pull?"

"Yeah, just one apiece, not the full thing."

"I'm not sure what we're talking about."

"The tarot," she said. "Thirty minutes is minimum to get anywhere. Enough time for a couple of questions. An hour's better. But some folks just want one card, so I pull one. Is something on your mind? I can give you a pull. You look a little troubled."

"I am," Mick said. "But then, who ain't? Thank you for the offer, but I can't do it on duty. Can you think of any reason Mrs. Morris called about you?"

"She doesn't like me."

"I got that impression. Why not?"

"I don't know for sure. Ronnie is the youngest of six kids. I think Molly is afraid I'll take him off somewhere. You know, make him move."

"Do y'all talk about moving?"

"No, never. I like it here. I'm from Maysville and couldn't wait to get away from there."

"I understand that," he said.

"You're from Maysville?"

"No, I'm from right here in Eldridge County. I left for twenty years."

"Then came back to be sheriff?"

"Not exactly. It's a long story."

"You sure I can't give you a reading? Or a one-card pull to get you through the day?"

"I'm sure," he said. "But you can let me take a peek inside so I can tell Mrs. Morris I did."

Loretta stood and pulled the bearskin aside. The interior was lit by several garlands of small white lights attached to electrical wires. A strong cedar smell came from a clump of dried boughs tied together and hanging from the high domed ceiling. Mick had the sensation of standing inside a Christmas tree. The single room was tidy and furnished with a bed, couch, small table, two chairs, and a dresser. A carpet lay on a raised plywood floor.

Several empty jars stood on a workbench beside a two-gallon jar of clumpy brown liquid. On the table were smaller containers with a metal armature on the neck designed to hold a cork in place. A funnel protruded from one.

"You caught me in the middle," Loretta said.

"Middle of what?"

"The big mama is ready for action. I'm making kombucha. You ever try it?"

"Is it like beer?"

"No," Loretta said. "It's filled with probiotics and anti-oxidants. Real good for you."

She used a spatula to lift a ragged disc of brown gunk from the big jar. It dripped a viscous fluid.

"This is the scoby," she said. "I call it the big mama. It gives birth to all the rest."

"I see."

"I jar up honey, too. Been trying lip balm but it's hard to fool with. I sell and trade, you know, at outdoor markets. Mount Sterling Court Day and Poppy Mountain. Anywhere folks get together. I used to do hooping but people didn't go for it."

She pointed to three brightly colored hula hoops leaning against a support post.

"I still keep my chops," she said. "Ronnie tried juggling but got bored."

"Where is Ronnie?"

"Out hunting work. Said he's got a line on a construction crew. He had a delivery job on a beer truck but quit after he found a dead man. Maybe if they catch the guy who did it, Ronnie'll go back to it. Y'all got any, you know, leads?"

"Not that I know of," Mick said. "I appreciate your time."

"Hey, let me give you some kombucha. Good for stress."

"No, thank you. I can't accept gifts."

"Oh, right. Come back when you're not the sheriff."

"Problem is," he said, "I'm always the sheriff."

Mick walked back to the front yard. Jonquils beside the porch steps had bloomed and the petals fallen, leaving clumps of green blades like fat scallions. Mick knocked at the door. Mrs. Morris opened it immediately as if waiting for him. She was smoking another cigarette, a different brand this time, long and skinny. Less tobacco, Mick thought, but more paper.

"Well," Mrs. Morris said. "Did you arrest her or give her a warning?"

"Mind if we sit down a minute?"

Mrs. Morris brightened momentarily and ushered him to a pair of wooden chairs on the porch. Mick wondered if the absence of a third chair was a deliberate insult aimed at Loretta.

"Mrs. Morris," he said.

"You can call me Molly if you want."

"Yes, ma'am. The way I see it, Loretta's not doing anything illegal."

"People come and go, night and day. Sometimes men when Ronnie's gone. They don't stay long. That ain't right."

"Near as I can tell, she's doing what she can to make a little money. Sells honey and some kind of health drink. Reads tarot cards."

"I don't hold with that bull puckey," she said. "The devil's pasteboards is what it is."

"It's not against the law and it doesn't hurt anybody. Same as looking at your astrology in a magazine. It gives folks comfort. We all need that."

"That's what church is for."

Mick nodded silently, waiting for the subject to dwindle. Everybody had a right to believe what they liked and nobody ever won a debate along those lines.

"Ma'am," he said. "Loretta thinks maybe you don't like her."

"She's right. I don't."

"Why is that?"

Mrs. Morris snorted in judgment and sucked on the cigarette like a hungry baby with a bottle. She blew a fierce strand of smoke in a straight line, then quickly took another long inhale. Her style of smoking was as dramatic as he'd ever seen.

"Listen a minute, Mrs. Morris," he said. "You called the station three times. I'm here and now you're holding back. It's against the law to make a false accusation, like your daughter-in-law selling dope or turning tricks out of a yurt. I've got real crimes to deal with. And lying to the law is one. So you'd best tell me why I'm really here."

"It's my sister," she said.

"Is Loretta bothering her?"

"No, nothing like that. When we were little my sister started fooling with a Ouija board. It messed her up something awful. Didn't do her one bit of good. I don't want that to happen to Ronnie."

"I didn't see a Ouija board in there."

"She does that damn tarot."

"I'm no expert," Mick said. "But it ain't the same. Ouija is about dead folks. Tarot is about the living person. Nothing spooky about it."

"I wouldn't know."

"Here's what I suggest, Mrs. Morris. Ask Loretta to give you a reading. She can do it right here on the porch. That way you'll know what she's up to. I don't think she's a bad person. Give her a chance."

Mick went to the county vehicle, weary of being sheriff. He was a homicide investigator, not a family drama interventionist. He wanted to turn on the light bar, crank up the siren, and drive out of state any direction, just go for days as fast as he could. Instead, he drove the speed limit and headed toward the Kissicks' house to visit his sister.

He wished he'd told Mrs. Morris that the Ouija board was nothing more than cardboard and plastic made in a factory owned by Hasbro, the largest board game manufacturer in the USA. Mick's closest buddy in boot camp had worked in the Massachusetts warehouse as a forklift driver. Alex turned a corner too fast with a full load of flat boxes loaded with a game called Risk. The forklift tipped and he dumped eighteen thousand tiny cubes that skittered across the cement floor. Alex got fired on the spot and enlisted the next day. He said that if he got killed in combat, Mick could go to the warehouse and visit him through a Ouija board, but he'd have to pick the right one since there were thousands in stock. At nineteen, they laughed at the absurd notion of mortality, then cleaned their rifles. A year later Alex died in Iraq.

Mick radioed dispatch and reached Sandra at the sheriff station. He told her he'd completed the Morris call and gave her his current location.

"You bringing Loretta in?" she said.

"No. Next time Molly Morris calls, you tell her we're not sending anyone out unless somebody is bleeding."

"Ten-four," she said. "That was my mom's attitude about taking us to the doctor."

"Better not tell Mrs. Morris that. She might take it as an excuse to stab somebody."

"Molly? If she was a stabber, she'd have got her ex-husband years ago. What's the story on Loretta?"

"One of these newfangled hippies, near as I can tell. Harmless and naive. I'm going to check on Linda."

Mick drove along the winding road. There was no center stripe or shoulder. Both sides of the narrow blacktop ended at a strip of weedy grass beyond which grew the heavy growth of the Daniel Boone National Forest. Half of what Mick knew, he'd learned alone in the woods. The rest came from war zones.

He slowed for a turn onto a county road and drove in
the middle to avoid scraping his vehicle against the low-
hanging branches of willow and maple. Their thick trunks
and lush limbs indicated underground water. He parked at
a house belonging to Shifty Kissick, a woman in her fifties who'd spent time with Mick's father in their mutual
youth. She'd married another man and had five kids, three
deceased. Her oldest son, Raymond, lived with her now.
Raymond was a Marine who'd recently come home from
Camp Pendleton in California, accompanied by his partner
Juan Carlos. They operated a taco truck six days a week and
made a good living.

Ostensibly they'd returned to look after Shifty, but Mick
believed if anyone in the world did not need personal care, it
was her. Shifty's nickname came from the homemade shifts
she'd worn as a child, a habit she still maintained. The only
difference was size, quality of fabric, and the pocket Shifty
sewed in place to accommodate a small-caliber pistol. The
right side of all her dresses hung low from the weight of
the gun. She'd taken in Mick's sister after Linda got hurt
on the job. They'd bonded at the hospital, and Shifty's
house had enough room for the bulky rehab equipment.

Mick sat in the official sheriff's SUV pondering how
his life had reached its nadir at age forty—a job he didn't
want, a car he didn't own, living in his dead mother's house,
divorced, adrift, and befuddled. It was a bad way to be and
he wasn't sure how to repair it. A few months back he'd
resigned from the US Army, having served with distinction

and received significant decoration, including the Soldier's Medal and the Silver Star. Now he preferred to sit in his vehicle, wishing he could avoid entering the potential maelstrom of Shifty and his sister Linda, two peas in an angry pod. He knew how to circumvent a trip line that ignited a homemade bomb made of gasoline and metal shards, but not how to talk to people he cared about. That trait had cost his marriage.

Mick left the SUV, crossed the yard to the porch, tapped on the screen door, and entered. A pervasive tension spread like lava throughout the house. Shifty sat in her chair facing a TV tuned to a monster truck rally. She gave him a baleful glance, then looked away. He could hear the clatter and clank of Linda working an elliptical machine for her wounded leg.

"Hidy, Shifty," Mick said.

"Just what we need," she said. "Another man broody as an old hen."

Mick walked down a hall to a large room that served as kitchen, pantry, dining area, and now a mini gym with a stationary bike and an elliptical machine. Sweating profusely, Linda worked the machine or it worked her, Mick was never quite sure of the process. Earbuds ran to her phone, which was mounted on the control screen. She watched a movie, undoubtedly one of her beloved romantic comedies in which an unlikely couple persevered after initial misperceptions of each other followed by many obstacles. Mick hated them.

He moved into her vision. Without missing a stroke in her stride, she waved him away.

"Not now," she said.

He dutifully left the kitchen. From the second floor came a sudden, rapid stream of Spanish, shrill and angry. Mick moved to the foot of the staircase. Juan Carlos continued to shout, his voice rising to a crescendo, then stopping. Raymond's response was pitched too low for Mick to understand. Shifty increased the TV volume until the whining roar of absurdly oversized vehicles drowned the argument. Mick abruptly wished he was enclosed in the silent yurt, or better—sleeping in a tent in the desert. At least in that situation he knew how to react.

He went outside and sat on the porch. The late May trees were fully leafed out and bright green, each leaf like a hand cupped toward the sky. Spring's optimism had shifted to the eager cheer of early summer. Heat and gravity hadn't yet begun to droop the vivid foliage. Mick recalled the first time he sat in the same spot a few years back, drinking coffee with Shifty and watching a chicken walk backward. He'd been married and planning retirement. Shifty had given him sausage on a biscuit, the single food he'd missed most during years of deployment. They'd gotten along fine until he later learned she'd lied through her teeth about every subject except the chicken.

He rested on the porch, mentally going through the future paperwork from the trip to the Morris house. Anticipating the effort was an old trick that made the actual task simple and fast. The words were already composed in his mind, he just had to transcribe them. The sound of heavy boots came down the steps inside the house, followed by rising Spanish. The screen door slammed open, hit the exterior wall, and bounced back. Raymond deflected it as he strode out carrying a government-issue Marine Corps seabag. He ignored Mick and marched across the yard. Behind him came Juan Carlos in shorts and a T-shirt, his face flushed with anger.

"¡Sigue! ¡Vamos! ¡Nunca vuelvas! ¡Estúpido! ¡Gilipollas! ¡Sal ahora!"

Raymond continued in a double-time march across the yard to the road, handling the stuffed seabag as if it were a loaf of bread. The sun dulled the military tattoos on his massive forearms. Mick wanted to follow but remained still to avoid drawing the ferocity of Juan Carlos. He suddenly remembered the backward-walking chicken's name—Sparky—and grinned. Juan Carlos saw the expression and spun to Mick.

"No te rías de mí," Juan Carlos said. "¡Cabrón!"

"Hola, amigo," Mick said.

"Take him and go," Juan Carlos said. "I like your sister more!"

"Tell her I said hidy."

Mick stood and left the porch, wary as an admonished dog. At the SUV he turned to face the house. Shifty had joined Juan Carlos. The combined force of their mutual glare traveled across the grass and bounced off Mick's face. He began driving toward town. He was surprised by the distance Raymond had traveled on foot and wondered vaguely if a Marine march was faster than the Army's. Mick passed Raymond and stopped in the middle of the road. With the fluid motion of a tai chi master, Raymond opened the door, tossed his seabag in the back, and climbed into the passenger seat. He stared straight ahead, breathing calmly despite the exertion. Mick put the SUV in gear and cruised forward.

"J. C. seems good," Mick said.

"Fuck you."

"He called me a *cabrón*."

Raymond grunted.

"What's it mean?" Mick said.

"You're a bastard. Maybe a goat."

"Both?"

"I don't fucking know, dude. It's not good. He called me a dickhead or a douchebag."

"That's worse," Mick said. "You want to stay with me?"

Raymond grunted assent and Mick drove to his sister's house in town. A stoplight halted them beside a drugstore. A few years ago, the parking lot had been notorious as a buy-site for prescription OxyContin. Now it was empty save for a few cars with older men behind the wheel, waiting for a family member. Old-time countrymen never entered a store.

A large church on the corner had been converted to a health care facility. Lightning had struck the steeple three times, prompting people to say that God was mad at the church. They overlooked the fact that the steeple was on top of a hill that was the highest point in Rocksalt. Mick turned onto Lyons Avenue, a narrow residential street that ended at Linda's house. Due to a steep hill, a creek, and a cemetery, Lyons was the last dead end in town. All the rest had been linked for development. Mick had lived in the house until he was eight. His parents divorced and he went to his grandfather's cabin deep in the hills. Linda stayed with their mom and eventually inherited the house.

Mick and Raymond entered the carport door and went through the kitchen to the living room. Multiple shelves held twenty-two clocks, with eight more hanging from the walls.

"Mom's," Mick said. "There used to be calendars in every room but Linda got rid of them."

"Where do I bunk?"

"Linda's room or the couch."

"Does she have a gun safe?"

"No. Why?"

Raymond hefted the seabag in answer, then sat wearily on the couch.

"Ditty kit," he said, "change of clothes. The rest is ordnance."

"Don't worry about it. Nobody'll break into the sheriff's house."

Mick sat in one of two large, lumpy chairs from the nineties. A reading light with a crooked shade had a built-in shelf that was covered in coffee rings.

"What happened?" Mick said.

"Me, I guess."

"That doesn't exactly clear the air."

"The past twenty years I lived alone or with a bunch of jarheads."

Mick waited but Raymond shook his head silently as if to himself.

"If you're going to stay here," Mick said, "I need to know more in case it has to do with Linda. You been living with her, too."

"I'm not saying nothing against your sister, Mommy, or J. C."

"But . . ."

"In a nutshell, I got on their nerves. Not all at once, but first one, then the other. Then they all three banded together and got mad at me. Soon as that went away, I'd piss off the next one. They all got mad again. Over and over. Pretty soon they were mad at me day and night, like in shifts. I spent most of my time on the porch."

"What about the food truck?"

"I think J. C. fired me."

"You think?"

"I didn't catch all the Spanish, but yeah. I'm pretty sure."

Mick started laughing. Raymond gave him a quick, hard look, then relaxed and giggled. It was a high-pitched sound that tickled Mick, who realized he'd never heard Raymond laugh before. The sound was incongruous with the black ops veteran sitting on the couch, his shaved head resembling a giant bullet.

"You need a job?" Mick said. "Deputy position is still open."

"Johnny Boy not coming back?"

"I can't talk about that," Mick said. "But if I don't fill the position, the mayor and judge will start angling to put their own deputy in."

"When do I start?"

"Right now. We'll go to the station and Sandra will give you a badge. You can have a state-issue pistol or use your own. Got one?"

"Yeah," Raymond said. "I got four."

"Pick one and let's go."

Ray-Ray nodded and stood, the expression on his face that of a Marine with a mission. They left and drove to the sheriff station.

Chapter Three

Mick parked in the blacktop lot, backing into the spot in case he needed to leave fast. A late-model Ford with a car seat was at the far edge. The only other car was a red Miata that belonged to Sandra Caldwell. She'd worked a couple of years as dispatcher, lately serving as unofficial adviser to Mick in the intricate ways of the civilian world. Their brief romantic history had been thwarted by Mick's new job. He couldn't legally date a subordinate and wouldn't ethically anyhow. Part of him was glad to avoid the emotional vulnerability. On the other hand he was lonely as the last leaf on a tree in winter.

Mick and Raymond entered through the tinted glass door. Sandra's desk was actually two metal desks set end to end with an old computer, a fax machine, a printer, and a landline telephone with a built-in crescent to prop on her shoulder. She faced an open laptop while talking on a cell phone. Another cell phone lay on the desk beside a stack of files. As she listened to the caller, she nodded and rolled her eyes.

"Yes, ma'am," she said. "I'll notify the sheriff."

She ended the call and rushed around the desk.

"Ray-Ray!" she said.

She and Raymond hugged briefly and she stepped back, looking him over.

"What brings you in here? A taco crime spree?"

"New deputy," Mick said. "He needs a badge and all the forms submitted to the county and state."

"Start date?" she said.

"Now."

"That's sudden," she said. "Did something happen?"

Mick and Raymond stayed silent.

"Yep," she said. "Something not good. Mick, I need to talk to you."

"Later," he said. "Take care of Raymond first."

"Now's better," she said. "It's important."

Mick nodded and walked past her desk toward his office door, which was still emblazoned with his sister's name.

"Wait," Sandra said. "Wait!"

The door was ajar and he pushed it open. Sitting in the guest chair was his ex-wife, Peggy. He'd last seen her more than two years ago when he dropped off divorce papers at her new house in Owingsville. It was an uneager task on his part, procrastinated for months, that ultimately left him feeling like a failure. Worse, it had pleased her, which plowed him under with sadness. Divorce made her happy and confident. She'd remarried and had two kids.

"Hey," he said.

"Mick," she said.

He closed the door, moved past her to his desk, and sat. Abruptly he saw the office through her eyes and realized he'd put nothing of his own in the room. A flag of Kentucky hung from a post in the corner. The walls held a large photograph of the governor and several framed certificates of merit, a room for the serious business of law enforcement. With a sense of dismay he realized that if Peggy was here, she had a problem and he'd try to help. Love didn't have an on/off switch. He wondered if it was him or the way of the hills.

They looked at each other. After a few seconds they spoke simultaneously: "You look good." Despite the banality, they laughed. It was an old trait of theirs, saying the same thing at the same time. They'd thought it was a sign that they were an ideal couple.

"How are your kids?" he said.

"Good, real good. Growing. Ruby is almost four and Jimmy Z. is walking now."

Mick nodded. It would be appropriate to inquire about her husband but he couldn't bring himself to do it. She'd gotten pregnant by Zack Jones while she was married to Mick. He studied her carefully. She'd put herself together for the trip to Rocksalt but she was distraught, a barely controlled tension in her posture and face.

"What's wrong, Peggy?" he said gently.

"I don't know what to do. I didn't want to come here but I didn't know where else to go."

"I'll do what I can."

"I know," she said. "That's why I didn't want to ask."

Mick nodded. There it was, he thought, the key to their marriage and its demise. Peggy had never asked him for anything so he'd given her everything. They'd never disagreed, never fought, never talked. They'd met young and spent their time going along with each other until eventually they'd each gone on alone.

"Are you in trouble?" Mick said.

"Not me. Zack is."

"What kind of trouble?"

"He's in jail."

"What's the charge?"

"They say he killed somebody."

"In Bath County?"

"He didn't kill anybody anywhere."

"I understand," Mick said. "I mean is he in the Bath County Jail?"

"No. He's here in Rocksalt."

"What do the police say?"

"Not much. At least not to me."

"Okay," he said. "I'll see what I can find out. Do you need anything? Water or food?"

"I can't stay," she said. "The kids are with Mom."

"She doing all right?"

"Same as ever. That's why I can't leave them very long."

"Are you still at the same number?" he said.

"Yes."

"Okay. I'll look into it and call you."

Relief passed over her face and for a moment he worried that she might cry. He'd only seen her cry once, the day they got married twenty-one years before. It had disarmed him and he hoped she wouldn't cry now.

"How's Linda?" she said.

"Her leg's getting stronger. She's got two machines and is on them half the day."

"Her place is pretty small."

"She's living at the Kissicks," Mick said. "More space. It's best with me working."

"Which Kissicks?"

"Shifty," Mick said.

"That woman is tough as woodpecker lips."

"So's Linda. They're a good match."

"We were, too," she said. "For a while."

Mick nodded. Discomfort swept over him. He stood, opened the door, and followed her out. Sandra and Raymond remained intent on their work, neither looking up. Mick ignored them and opened the exterior door for Peggy. She walked to the Ford with the car seat. He turned away—not his wife, not his kids, no reason to watch her hips. He wanted to harden his heart but didn't know how. He wondered if he could ever open it to someone else.

Inside the office, Sandra and Raymond looked at him expectantly.

"Her husband's locked up," Mick said. "Sandra, you know anything about it?"

"Zack Jones," she said. "The city police brought him in yesterday."

"Thanks. I'm going to go find out what I can. Is Raymond all set?"

"Yep. Acting deputy till the paperwork goes through. All we need is a vehicle."

Mick lifted his eyebrows to Raymond in a silent question.

"J. C. uses my car," Raymond said. "He needs it to get supplies for the taco truck. Mommy's old rig can barely make it across the county."

"I'll drive my pickup," Mick said. "You can have Linda's SUV."

"Linda might not like it."

"Doesn't matter. She's not the sheriff. You'll have to run me back to her place for my truck."

"Is that an order?"

"Did Sandra give you the badge yet?"

Raymond lifted his shirt to show the badge clipped to his belt.

"Then, yes, Deputy," Mick said. "It's a damn order."

Sandra laughed.

"Good luck, Ray-Ray," she said.

They went outside and Mick got in the passenger side. Raymond drove through town and up Lyons Avenue.

"You sure about this?" Mick said. "Being deputy?"

"No," Raymond said. "Are you?"

"I ain't been sure of a damn thing since I left the army."

"I hear you, dude."

"Dude. You were in California too long."

They both grinned briefly, then didn't speak the rest of the way. At Linda's, Mick started the 1963 Stepside pickup truck that had belonged to his grandfather. After letting the engine warm up a few minutes, he drove to the Rocksalt police station to see Chief Logan. When Mick was a kid, the police were housed on Main Street between a barber shop and a pool hall. They'd recently moved to the old post office, the grandest building on Main Street, and Mick realized he wasn't sure where the new post office was.

Chief Logan was on the phone and Mick waited on a bench in the broad hall tiled with 1930s-style tessellated shapes. He recalled seeing an old mural here from the same era and hoped it hadn't been painted over during renovation. A young secretary escorted Mick into the chief's office. He remained sitting, which meant his bad hip was bothering him. Chet Logan was in his fifties, had moved up through the ranks after being shot on the job, and was now considered the best chief in decades.

"Hidy, Mick," he said. "How's Linda?"

"Improving."

"Good. She'll be back to work soon."

"Not soon enough, Chet. I don't know how she does it. This week I had an escaped horse, three stray dogs, and four mailboxes knocked off their posts. The capper was a woman making kombucha in a yurt."

"I don't know what that means and don't want to know."

"One thing you need to know. Raymond Kissick is my deputy now."

"Good gosh almighty," Chet said. "A Kissick with a badge. What can I do for you?"

"Zack Jones."

Chet opened a manila folder on his desk, glanced over it, then spoke.

"Lives in Owingsville. Works at Lowe's. Clean record except for a DUI eight years ago. We're holding him in connection with the murder of Marlowe Martin, went by Skeeter. Age forty-eight. Owner of Ajax Bar and Grill. Liquor delivery guys found the body."

"Ajax," Mick said. "Ain't that in the county, not town?"

"Sure is. He was in the parking lot. The lot's in Rocksalt."

"Seems odd."

"It's all tied up with the alcohol laws. Skeeter was smart. He built that place right on the line, just out of our jurisdiction. People drank in there. We knew it. But Skeeter kept a tight lid on trouble. Any hint of a problem and he threw people out in the lot—city jurisdiction. He made sure they knew they were in Rocksalt and we'd be there fast."

"Get many calls?"

"Two this year. Minor wrecks by drunks. Last year, one theft."

"Out of a car?"

"Yep, a six-foot stuffed rabbit. Some kind of Easter decoration a guy won in a raffle. It was in the back seat. He had the window down for the ears to stick out."

"Somebody stole the rabbit?"

"His brother did. Said it was a joke but they never got along. A month later one brother shot the other over a woman. By the time we got there, they were laughing. No charges pressed."

"Nothing since?"

"Nope, they're both living with that woman. I don't know their arrangement and don't want to know."

"What happened to the giant rabbit?"

"Don't know that either."

Chet's landline made a sound and he pressed a button to route the call back to his secretary. A few seconds later, the cell phone on his desk started vibrating. Chet checked the caller and shook his head.

"The damn mayor," he said. "He's the worst one yet. But I said that about the last two. What's your interest in this homicide, Mick? Bored?"

"Zack Jones is married to my ex-wife. She asked me to look into it."

"Shoot," Chet said. "I knew Peggy moved to Owingsville but didn't put it together with Jones. What do you want to know?"

"Is he under arrest?"

"No, detained for another twenty-four hours. Then we'll bring charges. It doesn't look good, Mick. He's in a band that plays at Ajax. Word is, Skeeter owed the band money. Him and Jones got into it the other night. Big argument at the bar. Plenty of witnesses. Next day, Skeeter's dead. He had an old-time safe. It was wide open and empty. Looks like a robbery that Skeeter walked in on."

"Any evidence that he fought back?"

"Nothing. We found a gun in Skeeter's desk. Had dust on it."

"Hadn't been moved?" Mick said.

"Not in a long time. Skeeter was shot three times. My guess is a thirty-eight but waiting on Marquis to confirm. He's backed up at the funeral home. Some family had a die-off. Four of them in one week."

"Jones got a thirty-eight?"

"We searched the house and didn't find anything. No gun, ammo, or cleaning kit. Jones said he got rid of a shotgun and rifle when the second baby was born. His wife confirms that. Peggy, I mean. Sorry, Mick."

"What's his alibi?"

"A little vague," Chet said. "Claimed he went home late. Peggy didn't hear him come in and doesn't know what time it was. She goes to bed early on account of the kids."

"You looking at anyone else?"

"The rest of Jones's band. I hate fooling with musicians. Hard to keep them on topic. They're a drifty bunch. Either stoned or got the can't-help-its."

"Was Skeeter married?" Mick said.

"Divorced thirty years ago. One daughter living in Hawaii. Near as we can tell, he had relations with damn near every woman who worked at Ajax and half the customers. Not a one has anything bad to say about him. I mean none of them."

"Unusual."

"I wouldn't know. I married the first girl I kissed and been happy ever since. Sorry, Mick. I don't know what's wrong with me today. Saying the wrong thing since breakfast. That's why I don't want to talk to the mayor."

"You think Skeeter was shot in the parking lot?"

"Looks that way. A lot of blood. Too much for the body to have got moved there."

Mick nodded and stood.

"Thanks, Chet."

"Anything, Mick. Always ready to cooperate with your office. Did it with Linda. Any word on Johnny Boy?"

"Naw, still up in Indiana. Could I get copies of the crime scene photos?"

Chet picked up his phone and instructed someone to make copies.

"Appreciate it," Mick said. "You mind if I talk to Jones?"

"You sure you want to do that?"

"Not really. I'm doing this for Peggy. I never could say no to her. Probably why we didn't make it."

"I'll put a call in to the jail."

The landline made a sound and Chet grimaced.

"I wish you'd stick around another hour. The mayor, he'd gut himself to save his own skin."

Mick nodded and left. The secretary stood beside a color printer, closing a large manila envelope. She handed it to him.

"Ask you something?" he said.

"Yes, of course."

"What happened to the mural that used to be in here? They paint it over?"

"No, sir. It's at the library. Hang on, I've got a brochure."

She rummaged in a lower desk drawer and handed him a trifold glossy pamphlet. He thanked her and went outside to read it on the broad granite steps. Frank Long had painted the mural in 1939 as part of Roosevelt's New Deal cultural program. The small reproduction depicted a gray-haired woman sitting on the porch of a log cabin reading a letter. Two men in overalls flanked her along with a dog, a cat, and a younger woman. Long's initial sketch was rejected on the grounds that the older woman was too fat and the young one was too pretty. The artist objected and wrote back, explaining that he lived in Kentucky and the portrayals were legitimate. Mick admired Frank Long for standing up to federal bigots who'd never set foot in the hills. The same idiotic hypocrisy still existed today.

He angrily crumpled the brochure and tossed the paper wad in the truck bed, hoping he wasn't taking his frustration out on the past. Three months ago he'd retired from the army with a plan to live on a French island, and here he was trapped like a mouse with no choice but to eat the cheese.

Chapter Four

Johnny Boy Tolliver, former deputy of Eldridge County, Kentucky, blinked himself awake just after dawn. Instinctively listening for birds, he heard the unfamiliar calls of rollers and orioles and the high-pitched whistling of red kites. The foreign sounds reminded him where he was—a one-room shack on the island of Corsica. The dwelling was very old, built of stone and wood, the exposed rafters showing shallow scallops from an axe wielded long ago.

He rose and used a two-burner ring to make coffee. Breakfast consisted of bread, cheese, and ham, all in small portions. He drank from a five-hundred-milliliter bottle filled with well water. The mineral content had upset his stomach for the first few days but he'd gotten accustomed to its thick taste. He had no choice. Everything was new and different, even the language, although French used the same alphabet as English.

He dressed and went outside, where long shadows lay across the scrubby land, cast by large rocks and short pines. He sat in a spindly chair and drank his coffee. Even the cup was different, larger than he preferred, nearly too round for one hand. As his mind gradually became more alert, he started formulating a plan for the day, a short list of nothing to do.

The first two weeks he'd slept more hours per day than ever in his life. He'd arrived exhausted from twenty-three hours of travel preceded by a night of no rest. Never having flown before, he'd felt exhilarated by the prospect, then terribly afraid of the long tube crammed with people, the entire undertaking a shocking defiance of gravity and physics. As a kid he'd learned about Orville and Wilbur Wright, brothers who ran a bicycle repair shop and invented the first flying machine. He'd marveled at the phenomenal act of faith the brothers had, a faith he didn't share on his own transatlantic flight. The other passengers reclined in slumber, their heads guarded by eye masks and headphones, beginning to awaken for the serving of food, then the descent into Paris. He changed planes and flew across the Mediterranean Sea to the island of Corsica. Johnny Boy didn't know which was worse—the long passage through darkness, or the low flight over water.

He walked out of the airport like a man clandestinely drugged, taking tentative steps to prevent stumbling, awkward with his luggage, exhausted and bewildered. The air was hot and humid, the only familiar aspect of the new environment. People spoke fast in guttural tones with little shift in expression. The cars were small, some resembling children's toys, parked on asphalt tinted a foreign gray. The blue sky was both darker and brighter than in the hills. He stared upward like a drowning man stretching his neck for air above the surface of water. He set his luggage down and swallowed the sky with his eyes.

An unknown chunk of time passed. The warm light sank into his skin. His limbs began to tingle as if each pore was coming alive and touching its neighbor, the fresh air filling his lungs. He lost track of where he was and who he was. He heard a plane begin its roaring ascent, then a distant seagull, and a car shifting gears. He became aware that a voice was near, repeating itself three times, then a fourth.

"Tolliver," the voice said.

Johnny Boy lowered his head from the sky. A small man in his forties stood in front of him, five feet seven at the most, thin, his posture straight. The face was aged, lines deeply embedded as if he was a farmer well past sixty. One hand was tucked inside the side pocket of a shirt that was too heavy for the heat.

"Tolliver," he said again.

The accent was odd, the emphasis on his name striking different syllables.

"Yes," Johnny Boy said.

"Who sent you?"

"Mick Hardin," the man said. "Follow."

"Who are you?"

"Sebastien."

The man turned away and began walking. Johnny Boy gathered his luggage with the tail end of his newfound strength and tried to match the man's pace but fell behind. Sebastien stopped twice to wait, then began walking again before Johnny Boy caught up. It was nearly a quarter mile to the man's car, a battered gray Renault parked at the far end of the lot as if deliberately tucked away. Sebastien unlocked the rear hatch and stepped aside, offering no assistance as Johnny Boy placed his suitcase in the back.

They drove north in silence. Carved out of the massive rock mountain, the road followed the sea. A low stone wall barricaded the cracked blacktop from the water. Sebastien drove very fast, concentrating fully on the effort. Occasionally a motorcycle passed them at enormous speed, flashing by like a loud insect dodging the quickness of a bird's beak. The road curved tightly with the contour of the earth, then dropped in a steep slope straight to a rocky coast. The traffic barriers were made of thick wood poles mounted on low posts. Sebastien shifted gears smoothly and often, steering with a gentle touch.

Johnny Boy's body was leaden but his mind had become reactivated by the sea. In Kentucky he'd never seen a body of water bigger than a lake. He felt nausea from the swerving of the car, combined with a weary lightheadedness. He was thirsty. As if reading his mind, Sebastien passed him a plastic bottle of water. Johnny Boy drank half and concentrated on a treeless promontory ahead, a technique to quell car sickness. A few miles later he spoke.

"Where are we?"

Sebastien didn't answer for so long that Johnny Boy wondered if the man hadn't heard him.

"The cap," Sebastien said. "Cap Corse."

Johnny Boy nodded as if that explained everything, although he understood nothing. All that mattered was that Sebastien knew their location and destination. Johnny Boy had nothing aside from hastily gathered articles of clothing, toiletries, and a few hundred dollars that Mick had given him. Now his life was in the hands of a stranger. Trust came hard in the hills of eastern Kentucky and Johnny Boy understood that his only option was to rely on a wiry man who seldom spoke.

The car slowed as Sebastien downshifted and turned inland, climbing a narrow road. A power line ran alongside, held in place by two tall poles set at angles that converged at the top. A metal brace shaped like an M held them together. Sebastien made another turn onto a one-lane road with a slight shoulder. Now and then he steered around rubble that had fallen down the slope. They were traveling through a dense forest of low trees. He drifted off in semi-sleep, awaking when the car slowed to pass through a tiny village, then onto an unpaved road. They were still climbing. The thick foliage dissipated and Johnny Boy could see an unfamiliar crop in scraps of flatland below. One more turn and Sebastien stopped at a small house built of stone. He left the car, retrieved the two pieces of luggage, and carried them to a heavy wooden door. He inserted a key, which he left in the lock. Johnny Boy followed him through the entrance to his new home.

Sebastien deposited the suitcases in the center of the room and pointed to a pantry laden with canned food, potatoes, cured ham, rice, and barley. A portable refrigerator hummed in a corner beside a sink. Through a parted curtain was a toilet. Sebastien gestured to a low bed.

"Sleep," he said. "Sleep now."

He walked out, closing the door, and Johnny Boy heard the Renault's engine start, then fade as it departed. Light filtered through thin curtains covering three windows. On a scarred table was a container of salt, a pepper mill, two tomatoes, a bowl of grapes, an orange, and a large bottle of water. Johnny Boy stumbled to the bed and lay down fully dressed. He awoke in the night, went to the bathroom, removed his boots and clothes, and lay back down.

For the next three days he barely moved or ate. He drank water and slept. Each time he awakened he had to reacquaint himself with his surroundings—the stone walls cool to the touch, the outside world of rock and shrub and short pine. He preferred the sweet escape of slumber to his own thoughts. Nothing seemed real, like a dream that maintained itself during brief periods of being awake. He'd been in one place and, overnight, was occupying another life as if teleported. It didn't make sense, although he knew the reasons for this abrupt shift. He owed Mick and now he owed Sebastien. But for what? What was the point of paying a debt when his life was not worth living? He went back to sleep.

Chapter Five

Mick drove east of town, determined to focus on the future instead of his own sad past. He loved the hills. He loved his grandfather's old truck. He loved birds and wildflowers. It occurred to him that he was adept at loving things that were incapable of loving him back. Maybe he didn't know how to encourage love or maintain it.

He passed the turnoff to Christy Creek, recalling the old drive-in movie theatre, now torn down and replaced by an elementary school. Farther on, he slowed for a wide curve that ran beside the huge lot of junk vehicles where his grandfather bought parts to repair the truck. Mick had accompanied him on those trips, roaming around the narrow dirt lanes, climbing on top of old cars, and passing Papaw tools to remove the necessary parts. The junkyard was gone now and the owner's son ran a lawnmower franchise on the site. Mick felt a sense of loss brought on by seeing Peggy. Driving the old pickup meant he was literally inside the past, encased by memory.

He drove more slowly, concentrating on the faded center stripe to avoid seeing more places that were gone—the barber shop, a mechanic's garage, a gigantic willow that had shaded the creek. The railroad crossing was paved over, the steel tracks peeled from the earth. Footpaths through the woods were overgrown by weeds. His grade school was gone except for the gym currently used as a community center for a place that had lost its community when the state shut the school. The road narrowed and twisted. He made a turn onto the remnants of a dirt lane that led to his grandfather's cabin where he'd grown up.

Two years ago the cabin was gutted by arson in an attack against Mick. The hewn log walls were over a hundred years old and had withstood the fire, leaving a shell with a charred interior. Everything else was destroyed. Mick had hired a construction crew for a full renovation, paying extra for a straight job, start to finish. He parked beside three trucks and a stack of lumber draped with a tarp. The new roof had heavy decking covered by green sheet metal. The porch was fully rebuilt. Carpenters were now replacing the window and door frames.

The boss glanced at Mick, gave some orders, then approached. Wendell was in his midthirties, slim and earnest. He'd been in construction since he was sixteen and

now ran his own small company. In his free time Wendell
hunted duck, often traveling out of state.

"Hidy, Mick," he said. "You doing all right?"

"Pretty good. Learned about kombucha today. You
hear of it?"

"Oh, yeah, my wife swears by it. Drinks a glass every
morning for her cholesterols. I think it tastes funny. Why?
You try it?"

The high-pitched sound of a circular saw stopped their
talking. It ended and Mick listened to the silence. The crew
had scared most of the birds and small animals away but
they returned every evening. Sometimes Mick came out
after dark to listen.

"Looks like it's coming along," Mick said.

"Yep. Plumbing and electric is about done. We'll have
the windows and doors in by tomorrow."

"Then what? Flooring?"

"That's right. It'll be here this week."

"Y'all are fast."

"Well," Wendell said. "Your place is pretty small.
We're over the worst of it. Getting new studs in against
the old walls was tough. Some of them logs are damn near
petrified, you ask me."

"Yeah, probably why they didn't burn. You'll be done
when? A week? Ten days?"

"Hope so. No promises. Still yet got the fixtures to set,
paint the drywall, put up the interior trim and paint it. Got
to work around the floor guys' schedule. After they're done,

it'll need a few days for the poly to dry. That'll depend on weather."

"Then what?" Mick said.

"Clean up. Pay up. Move in."

Wendell gave a quick grin, then sighed and looked around at the land. The house sat at the end of a ridge surrounded by heavy woods. The west side had a steep drop-off to a creek running through the holler.

"This is the prettiest place I ever worked," Wendell said.

"My great-grandpa picked it out."

"He had a good eye for land."

"What he was," Mick said, "was a man who wanted to be off on his own. His boy, my papaw, was the same way. My daddy tried town but it ate him up. He came back up here for a while and drank himself to death."

The sound of work had stopped and the four carpenters were staring at Wendell. Mick understood that they were being respectful, not wanting to interrupt their boss's conversation with the owner.

"Well," Wendell said, "I best go find out what's wrong. See ya."

"See ya," Mick said.

He got in the truck and drove back toward town. Renovation cost more than the house was worth but it was important to Mick. It was the only part of his past he could rebuild. Maybe that's why he'd come home to a place that was barely home.

He radioed Sandra, who informed him that Raymond was already on his first call, a trespasser at a barn on the old Sharkey Road. Mick ended transmission, wondering what his grandfather would think if he saw his pickup outfitted with an onboard GPS, miniature computer, and a two-way Motorola radio. He'd probably laugh at the absurdity, a habit he'd passed on to Mick.

He cruised through Rocksalt to the Sledge Funeral Home. The owner, Marquis Sledge III, was carrying on the family business begun in the 1970s. He doubled as county coroner, an elected position, which he won without opposition every four years. Marquis had gone to high school with Linda, who still called him "Marky Three," his teenage nickname.

Mick parked in the funeral home's empty lot, admiring the freshly painted stripes that indicated spots for cars. Each space was overly wide, a thoughtful touch for people who were bereaved and not thinking clearly. Inside, he greeted the receptionist, a woman over seventy who'd worked for all three generations of Sledges. Her loose dress was of a style that never went out of style. The only change was her hair—dyed a little too dark and permed like a helmet.

"Hidy, Miss Patton," he said. "Here to see Marquis."

"We're real busy, Sheriff."

She reached for a phone and Mick went down the hall, past large framed pictures of Marquis I and Marquis II. At the end was an office, the same one used by all the Sledges.

Marquis III's concession to the passage of time had been redecorating it in multiple variations of tan. Mick knocked at the open door and stepped inside.

"Hey, Mick," Marquis said. "How's Linda?"

"Ornery as hell. Frustrated. Mad."

"She's getting better then."

"Not soon enough to suit me."

"You don't like being sheriff?"

Mick sat in a guest chair. Above a couch was the only spot of color—an enlarged photograph of a cardinal, Kentucky's state bird. Mick tipped his head to it.

"I'd rather be that bird," he said.

"Short life," Marquis said. "About three years. If they lose their mate they find another one."

"Maybe I'll try that one day. Guess you got a line on available widows in the county."

"I didn't mean it that way."

"It was a joke."

"I see," Marquis said. "My business is too serious for jokes."

"Mine, too. That's why humor is necessary. Then again, maybe I'm not all that funny."

They looked at each other. Marquis was adept at silence, a crucial skill for a funeral director. His face always projected the calming combination of sympathy and distance. He wore a deliberately cheap suit to reassure his clients that he hadn't gotten above his raisings. His plain black shoes were never polished to a sheen. Mick remembered

Marquis's father occasionally wearing tasseled loafers that irritated people due to their fanciness.

"I'm here about Marlowe Martin," Mick said.

"It'll have to be quick. I've got a viewing service in an hour. That poor Anderson family. Lost four in a week. Don't see it that often this time of year. Usually winter, right around Christmas and New Year's. Nobody knows why."

Mick nodded and followed Marquis through a locked steel door into the morgue. Marquis opened a hatch built into the wall and slid out a heavy tray holding the remains of Marlowe Martin. He gestured to Mick, who peered carefully at the wounds.

"Three shots," Marquis said. "One in the left arm and one in the left side. That bullet nicked the kidney. The third went through the left lung into the heart."

"Any way to know which shots came first? The sequence?"

"Not really. The heart shot would have stopped him. So it's possible that the arm and side wounds were first."

"Time of death?"

"Roughly between 12:00 p.m. and 4:00 a.m. Two nights ago. He came in here the same day they found him."

"Defensive wounds?"

"No cuts or scrapes. Nothing under his nails. Two knuckles on his right hand are swollen. No fracture. Could be from a punch. Or he dropped something on it beforehand."

"Any chance the body was moved after death?"

"No scuff marks on his body. Clothes are clean enough. If he was moved, somebody carried him."

"He went by Skeeter," Mick said. "Did you know him?"

"No, I don't go out. Nobody wants to see a mortician in a bar or restaurant. Once a month I take my wife to Lexington to eat."

Mick nodded, thanked him, shook hands, and left. He walked past the large oil paintings of Marquis I and II, noting the empty space reserved for Marquis III. His reward for a life presiding over death would be a painting few people would look at.

Chapter Six

Mick drove across the county to examine the crime scene, telling himself that he needed as much information as possible before talking to Zack Jones. But the truth was simpler—he didn't want to see the man who'd had an affair with his wife. Mick and Peggy had gotten married young and lived apart for months at a time due to his military career. She'd never fit in with the transient community of army wives on base. He supposed their divorce was inevitable, but he'd rather go look at the parking lot where a man had died than talk to her new husband.

Kentucky has 120 counties, each a private fiefdom for politicians with a single law enforcement officer—the elected sheriff. Every county was designated wet or dry, which meant alcohol was legal or illegal. The Eldridge County bootlegger stayed in business by participating in church events, helping families that needed extra money, and contributing to various social causes. When necessary, he bribed the state police for prior notification of the occasional raid. This gave the bootlegger time to find a man who was willing to be arrested and get paid for serving jail time. The practice had diminished when alcohol was declared legal in town, but illegal everywhere in the county. The arrangement pleased most people—Rocksalt received income, the bootleggers stayed in business, and the preachers could rail against the evils of town as well as alcohol.

Mick's grandfather had told him about an old-time bootlegger in a log house that straddled the lines of two dry counties. Depending upon which sheriff showed up, he crossed the cabin floor to the other county and was safe from arrest. The sheriffs of the two adjoining counties never coordinated to arrive at the same time. In this fashion, the bootlegger made a fortune. He also became so fearful of arrest that he never left his home. Family members brought him food. He gained a tremendous amount of weight, had a fatal heart attack, and was too big to fit through the door. After much consternation, the sheriffs decided to lift the linked logs on one corner of the cabin and swing open the entire wall as if on a hinge. They moved the body out, then shut the wall back in place.

Ajax Bar and Grill sat six inches out of the town limits in the far edge of the county. When the wet vote passed for town, the owner bulldozed a large parking lot in front of the entrance—deliberately within Rocksalt. Before Mick's sister became sheriff, her predecessor periodically received a bundle of cash to leave the place alone. Linda had refused the money but continued to let Ajax be Ajax. People needed a place to drink, she said, and the county had bigger problems than a few drunks.

Mick parked on the shoulder and walked the perimeter of the parking lot. There were no cars. The gravel was sparse in places with dry mud holes and deep ruts. His movements slowed to a somnolent pace as he held the crime scene photos and shifted position to ascertain their point of view. Skeeter's body had lain face down, slightly to the left of the tavern's entrance. In the photographs, the corners of the building slanted to the sky, which meant a slight wide-angle lens. Mick moved a few steps to accommodate the distortion. He placed the picture in the gravel. He stepped back and squatted to gain a sense of the shot's angle, using the front door for reference. He moved the photo, then repositioned it to match the orientation of the body. To guard against any wind, he weighted the corners of the photograph with rocks.

Satisfied, he withdrew his cell phone and called Chief Logan, who answered immediately.

"Mick," he said.

"Did Skeeter have a vehicle in the parking lot?"

"Yeah, he drove one of those new Mustangs you can barely see out of. I don't like them. Give me a '67 ragtop any time."

"Where was it parked?"

"Hang on a minute, I'll check the file."

Mick waited, studying the building. A rusty dumpster stood at one edge, shaded by a large maple. A finch flew from the tree as if cutting a yellow stripe in the air. Chet came back on the line.

"Skeeter's car was on the south side, close to the bar. He always parked there."

"Where is it now?"

"Impound lot. We searched it. Nothing. He kept a real clean car."

"Was there blood at the scene?" Mick said.

"Yes, quite a bit where he was laying."

"Was there blood anywhere else?"

"None we found. There was a lot of people. Foot traffic, cars, ambulance. Delivery truck. Folks driving by stopped to see. A real mess."

"Any employees there?"

"One," Chet said. "Hammy Johnson. Late forties. Skeeter's right-hand man."

"He got a record?"

"Misdemeanor theft twenty-four years ago. Clean as a new stick pin since. I'll send his contact info."

"Thanks, Chet."

Mick ended the call. Based on the position of Skeeter's body, he was probably going toward his car when the fatal shot hit him. Mick wondered if Skeeter was fleeing, but the gravel was too scattered to gauge his pace by the length and weight of his footprints. Mick walked a slow, wide circle to

the front of the bar and studied the floorboards of the porch.
Dirt. Dust from gravel. The stains of spilled beer. Cigarette
butts and the black imprints where they'd been stepped on.

Carefully looking at the ground before each step, Mick
slowly moved away from the door toward Skeeter's parking place. The gray limestone gravel had been embedded
in the earth for years, enough time for the bottom of each
rock to become discolored. He bent his knees and tipped
forward at the waist, using a stick to turn over the brown
rocks and reveal the pale sides that had previously been facing the sky. He found one with a faint bloodstain. A few
feet farther he found another. As he approached the photo
on the ground that represented the position of the body, he
discovered three more small, bloody rocks. They formed
a curving path toward the spot where Skeeter's body had
been. Mick stood still and twisted from the waist, aiming
his vision to follow the blood trail. Skeeter had been shot,
then tried to escape to his vehicle. A final bullet in his back
had dropped him.

Skeeter died in the parking lot, which was city land.
But if he'd been initially shot in the bar, then the attack
would fall under the county sheriff's purview. Mick needed
to get inside the bar. Two small windows were on either
side of the door. One had a sign:

OPEN FOUR TO ONE. WEDNESDAY–SATURDAY.
MUST BE TWENTY-ONE TO ENTER.
NO CHECKS.

The front door was locked and he walked around the one-story building to the back. The rear area was dirt and grass filled with discarded debris—a collapsing stack of pine pallets, a fifty-gallon barrel half full of ashes, and the rusty front axle of a car. He searched the clumped fescue and horseweed, finding a few beer bottles and a stack of bricks with rough mortar still clinging to the edges. He suddenly recalled hours of chipping mortar off old bricks for his grandfather's plan to shore up the foundation of the shed. The bricks needed to be smooth to stack right, Papaw had said. Mick had gone to bed with swollen hands and raw fingers but felt triumphant for having completed the chore.

He refocused his mind and ranged farther into the overgrown area behind the bar. High grasses ran to a fence, beyond which grew a crop of feed corn. The tires of a car had pressed down two lines of weeds that were nearly back upright. Someone had parked here recently. He went to the driver's side and inspected the ground, finding four fresh cigarette butts. He picked them up by the burnt ends and tucked them away. Maybe the killer had waited here for Skeeter.

Chet had sent the employee's phone number and Mick called it. A man's voice answered.

"Shoot, it's your nickel."

Mick chuckled. He hadn't heard that phrase in a long time. It was a throwback to the early 1950s, when a phone call cost five cents. Mick introduced himself and asked the man to come and unlock Ajax. He went to the front and retrieved the photo from the lot.

Chapter Seven

Fifteen minutes later Hammy Johnson drove an F-150 into the lot and parked near the front. He had a loose-jointed, shambling walk and wore blue jeans, boots, a work shirt with the sleeves cut off, and a cap bearing the logo of Bluestone Speedway. A front tooth was missing and a cigarette was wedged into the gap, allowing him to talk and smoke without using his hands. It was resourceful and expedient, both typical traits of the hills.

"Bad business," Hammy said.

Mick nodded.

"I don't mean bad for the bar, but in general."

"I understand," Mick said. "It's bad all the way around. We're having trouble finding a next of kin to notify."

"He's got a grown girl in Hawaii. They weren't close. I told the chief."

"You work for Skeeter a long time?"

"Damn near long as I can remember. We grew up together. Did what we could to get a little cash. Cleared brush. Gathered walnuts. Hung burley at the tobacco warehouse. Loaded and unloaded ever what anybody needed."

"Nothing on the shady side?"

Mick watched the man's eyes carefully to see if he would lie.

"Once," Hammy said. "We took a bunch of copper out of an old house. Nobody'd lived in it for I don't know how long. We were nineteen, dumb as hell. Got caught. I went to jail on it."

"Not Skeeter?"

"Naw. The law knew he was part of it but I kept it to myself. Never told a soul till you."

"Why tell me?"

"Ol' Skeeter's dead. It don't matter now."

He stared at the spot where the body had been. Closing his lips around the cigarette, he inhaled deeply, then blew the smoke from one side of his mouth. His face held an expression of sadness, a sudden and terrible shift in his eyes, mouth, and jaw. Mick had seen the guilty sorrow of someone who'd murdered a friend and this wasn't it.

"Hammy and Skeeter," Mick said gently. "Y'all must've been wild back then."

Hammy grunted and smoked, hands at his sides.

"Where'd those nicknames come from anyhow?" Mick said.

"Well, Marlowe, he always moved fast, anything he did. Talked fast, too. Folks said he was quick as a mosquito, you know."

"A skeeter."

"Yep. He never slowed down, either. They started calling me Hammy because I liked ham when I was a kid. Couldn't get enough of it. Still can't. I eat it damn near every day. You ever have a nickname?"

"A few. None that took. There's a guy up in Detroit who calls me Shitbird. He's from down here. He goes by Shorty."

They stood nodding together, listening to a house wren cheerfully warn the world that this was its territory. The sound came from a cedar by the dumpster.

"Can you let me inside the bar?" Mick said.

Hammy dropped his chin once, squinting his left eye as the cigarette burned down. He plucked it from his teeth and flicked it away. Mick memorized where it landed, then followed Hammy to the front door. The interior smelled of beer and cigarettes. Hammy switched on a series of lights— overheads, a few sconces, and a bright spotlight aimed at the door. Mick remained still, letting his eyes adjust to the blend of brightness and shadow. He'd always envied owls for their ability to open and close each pupil on its own, a conscious and deliberate act that allowed the bird to see everything at once. Humans had to make do with squinting and peripheral vision. Owl prey never escaped.

The far corner held a low stage for bands. In front was an area for dancing with rows of tables against opposite walls. A battered bar had several mismatched stools. Behind it were two shelves for liquor—bourbon and vodka with two bottles of rum on one end. Large taps dispensed two kinds of cheap draft beer. Streaks of dried water lay in swirls on the floorboards. Hammy began wiping the surface of the bar by rote, reminding Mick of an anxious dog obsessively licking a nearby surface. Mick gestured to a closed door.

"What's down there?"

"Storeroom. Skeeter's office. Walk-in cooler. Closet. Back door."

"Can you show me?"

Hammy came around the bar, tapping a set of keys clipped to his belt. Beside it was a folding knife in a case. A chain from a belt loop to a long wallet protruded from his back pocket. Hammy inserted the key and frowned.

"Supposed to be locked," he said. "But it ain't."

The door opened inward. Mick flicked a wall switch for an overhead light, stepped inside, and shut the door. The back of the door had a thick splotch of dried blood. Mick photographed it, understanding that the town police had left the door open, and never checked behind it. Hammy followed him down the dim hall. A storage closet contained a bucket on wheels with a mop, a push broom, and cleaning liquid. The walk-in cooler held stacks of beer.

Hammy opened Skeeter's office and stepped back as if in respect. Mick was surprised by the décor, which was in stark contrast to the rest of the tavern. A vintage oval rug with scalloped edges had a floral pattern of green, black, and accents of yellow. There was a plush blue couch with tasteful pillows leaning against the armrests. The walls held three framed reproductions of paintings that Mick recognized as Impressionism. In a corner was an antique roll top desk with a built-in blotter pad and numerous cubbyholes. Behind the door was a hook with two clean shirts and a pair of trousers on hangers.

Mick stood in the center of the room and turned three times, taking everything in. It had the feel of an antique shop or the boudoir of an elderly European. The only item that seemed to fit the office of a bar owner was a squat steel safe on wheels with the door wide open. It was empty.

"Do you know the combination to the safe?" Mick said.

"Nope. The only secret he kept from me."

"Why would he do that?"

"He said the safe was the one thing he had all to himself in the world. And nothing inside had to do with me or the bar. I done told the town law every bit of this. I didn't open the safe. I didn't kill Skeeter. And I didn't steal nothing off him."

"What'd he keep in there? Cash?"

"Don't think so. I seen it open once. There was just papers."

"What about paying the bills?"

"Old-school. Wrote a check and put it in the mail."

"Where's the checkbook?" Mick said.

"In the desk drawer where he kept it."

"Tell me how it works at closing."

"We close at one o'clock if there's business. Early if nobody's here."

"I understand," Mick said. "I mean, do you follow a procedure? Take me through the steps."

"The servers wipe the tables down and leave. I count the money and separate the credit card receipts. Put it all in a bank bag and give it to Skeeter. He added it up while I mopped the floor. Sometimes we had a beer and talked after."

"He was always here?"

"Yeah, he didn't think it was a good idea for one person to leave alone with money."

"Carry guns?"

"I did. We kept two pistols in his office. I took one with me when we left, brought it back the next day. A .41 Remington Magnum. Cops took it."

"Skeeter didn't carry a gun?"

"He kept a little snub-nose in his desk. I never knew him to have it on him. Cops took it."

Mick nodded. He ran through the facts as he knew them combined with what he'd observed outside. Skeeter had left after closing, then returned later and got killed. It was too loose a narrative. He needed to fill in gaps with concrete information.

"Did you find Skeeter?" Mick said.

"No, the delivery guys did. I came to work and the cops were here."

"Where were they?"

"Some outside. Some in the bar."

"Did you come in?"

"No way," Hammy said. "I wanted to leave but they made me stay outside."

"Did you let them in the bar?"

"They were already inside."

"What about in here? Skeeter's office."

"I don't know," Hammy said. "They didn't let me stay inside long. Just to see if anything was missing behind the bar. Nothing was."

"Who all had keys?"

"Me and Skeeter."

"When you left the other night," Mick said. "Was Skeeter's office locked?"

Hammy poked his bottom lip out in concentration and rolled both eyes up and to the right. Most memory was stored there, especially visual memory, and Mick understood he was trying to recall. If he'd looked to his upper left, he'd be inventing a realistic lie.

"Yep," he said. "Sure was. Why?"

"If the cops were in the bar when you got here, it was already unlocked. I'm wondering if his office was, too."

Hammy lifted his eyebrows in surprise. Mick closed the door and listened for a full minute, then opened the door. Hammy was standing in the same position like a vigilant dog.

"Is it my ears," Mick said, "or is this room really quiet?"

"Oh, yeah. Skeeter, he put some kind of acoustic panels in the walls."

"Why'd he do that?"

"Said a bad band got on his nerves."

"Could you hear if someone was in here with him?"

A sly grin spread across Hammy's face like a sudden stream of light from behind a heavy cloud. Just as quickly it was gone.

"My opinion, that was the main part of it. This little old room saw its share of action if you know what I mean."

"Uh-huh," Mick said. "Anyone in particular?"

"Naw. Skeeter, he'd fuck a glass of milk."

"What about married women? Some husband who might hold a grudge?"

"No, sir. He was real careful about that. Single, divorced, or widowed, he always said. But never married ones."

"What about age?"

"At least forty. Said young ones were too much drama. The older they were, the more they appreciated him."

Mick nodded. He'd heard that sort of thing before. They left the office, walked through the bar and outside. The sky had darkened to the north. In a matter of minutes, the air pressure had dropped. Hammy struck a wooden kitchen match against the zipper of his jeans, lit a cigarette, and wedged it into the gap between his teeth. He tossed the match into the lot. Mick hadn't seen any in the weeds around back.

"Always use those matches?" he said.

"Try to. Got it off my great-grandpa. He had a way of splitting one match in half with his thumbnail. Kept them in his shirt pocket. Said in the Depression, guys quartered them."

Distant thunder sounded, followed by a brief breeze. A light rain began hissing through the trees, one of Mick's favorite sounds. Each separate drop made a tiny pockmark in the dust of the lot.

"What're you going to do?" Mick said.

"Shut the bar down, I reckon. Everything's in his name. I don't know if I'm supposed to pay the bills or just lock it up and walk away."

"What do you want to do?"

"I don't know that either."

The rain stopped as quickly as it had begun, a quick shower that cooled the air momentarily but would raise the humidity. Still, Mick liked the way things looked now—every surface transformed to a miniature prism by the thin skim of water. Each leaf glowed on its own. The clouds suddenly parted and the vivid sunlight snapped everything to attention, as if the world was on full alert.

"Well," Mick said, "there's one more thing we need to talk about. You were here the other night, right? If you and Skeeter closed up, you were the last feller to see him."

"Reckon so."

"Was he all right?"

"Same as ever. Pretty steady in general."

"I heard there was a big to-do with one of the musicians."

Hammy sucked on the cigarette and spewed the smoke out of the corner of his mouth opposite from the missing tooth. Mick watched the pale tendrils dissipate in the breeze. Briefly the smoke encircled Hammy's head like a caul.

"Yeah," Hammy said. "Skeeter got into it with Zack Jones, plays bass in the Big Bigs. Dumbest name for a band I ever heard."

"What'd they get into it over?"

"Zack said Skeeter owed them money."

"Did he?"

"I don't know. The other guys thought so. Zack, he did all the talking for them. Said Skeeter owed them more money than he paid."

"What'd Skeeter say?"

"Said he didn't talk business in front of everybody. They should go back to his office and hash it out. Zack wouldn't go."

"Why not?"

"Said it was just a way for Skeeter to get him alone and talk him out of the money."

"Think that was true?" Mick said.

"Could be. Skeeter could be real convincing. But Zack wouldn't go with him. Just kept yelling for his money. I think he wanted people to know."

"Who all was there?"

"Me, a waitress, and the band. About three people finishing off their drinks. Most everybody left when the band quit playing."

"Anything physical?" Mick said. "Pushing, shoving, punches?"

"Naw. Neither one of them is that way. Zack, I doubt he'd fight a frog. And Skeeter had me if things got rough."

"You were ready?"

"Yeah, had my hands on a ball bat behind the bar. But all they did was holler and yell. Mainly Zack."

"Any threats? From a one of them?"

"Zack said they wouldn't play here again till they got paid. Said he'd tell everybody not to come here anymore. 'Boycott' was the word he used. Zack left mad."

"What about the rest of the band?"

"Ain't but three. They were about done packing their gear. Skeeter went to his office. I helped the drummer carry his cases to his car."

"Did the drummer have anything to say?"

"He lost his sunglasses. Asked me to keep an eye out for him."

Mick frowned and Hammy responded.

"He always wore them when he played. Said he had drummer eyes and didn't want nobody taking pictures of him like that. You can't stop people with a cell phone, so he wore sunglasses."

"I never heard of drummer eyes."

"Me neither. He closed them sometimes and thought they looked weird. Other times they rolled back in his head and all you could see was the white parts."

Hammy took one last hands-free pull on his cigarette, then tossed it into the lot.

"Anything else?" he said. "I got to get back to the house. My dog had pups. I'm worried about the runt. It's the prettiest one."

"How'd y'all pay the bands?"

"Tip jar and free beer for ones starting out. Some got a flat fee afterwards. The night Skeeter died there was a cover charge, three dollars to get in. The band got it all. Zack thought there was a lot more people there than the money Skeeter gave him."

"What do you think?"

"I don't count heads. My job is to keep the beer and liquor going."

"Who works the door?"

"Skeeter."

Mick nodded. The situation was loose enough to be corrupt, and if it was legitimate, loose enough for resentment and conflict.

"How much money are we talking about?" Mick said.

"One fifty, maybe two hundred."

"That ever happen before? A band thinking they ort to get paid more."

"Never. Skeeter, he was honest. Stayed on top of all the bills. Paid the workers every week."

"Any change recently in him? I mean on a personal level."

Hammy thought about it, pushing the tip of his tongue through the gap in his teeth. He squinted at the parking lot and took a big breath.

"Sort of," he said.

"Sort of."

"He was tense. Sometimes it was like he wasn't paying attention when we talked. I had to tell him things twice. He was there but not there. Like somebody who just smoked a joint, but Skeeter didn't smoke weed. I thought maybe he was thinking about something else. First time I ever seen that in him."

"What do you think was going on?"

"No idea, bub. Like I said, it was brand spanking new. He had something on his mind but I don't know what."

"Thanks."

"That mean I can go?"

"You can do what you want. I'm not keeping you here, Hammy. I'm trying to figure out who killed Skeeter."

Hammy locked the front door and lit another cigarette. Mick watched him walk toward his vehicle, a man who'd lost his job and best buddy. It showed in his slow gait, his slumped shoulders, and downturned head. A man worried about his dogs.

Hammy drove away and Mick picked up his discarded cigarette butt. As he expected, it didn't match the ones from the back of the bar. He walked around the building again, thinking about what he now knew and what he didn't. Some kind of paperwork was missing from the safe. He peered into the rusty yellow dumpster. The bags had been split open and searched, the contents tossed back in, probably by the town police. In the tree line he found a long stick that was still limber enough to remain intact. He leaned into the dumpster and used the stick to dig through the garbage. It was fruitless work. He realized that he was literally sifting trash to avoid interviewing his ex-wife's husband. The specter of his own cowardice propelled him across the lot to his truck.

Chapter Eight

Johnny Boy wasn't sure how many days passed until he awakened feeling capable of prolonged movement. He ate, made coffee, and resolved to step outside. A few clouds scudded lazily across the sky like boats drifting on water. A mountain strewn with loose rock rose behind the house. Out front were two large tree stumps and a pump protruding from the earth with a metal handle and a short hose. He went back to the house for soap, removed his clothes, and washed himself in the cold water. The sun dried his skin. He rinsed his shirt, pants, socks, and underwear, then placed them on a rock.

Back in the dim, cool air of the house, he dressed in fresh clothes and walked the curved dirt lane. It was uphill and ended at another single-story house with two additions built of wood. It faced away from the hard-slanting sun of day. In front was a small porch with a high ceiling. The road went around the house and Johnny Boy wondered if the

Renault was parked back there. He had no idea what to do. He took a standing rest. There was no motion other than a few birds circling high, no sound aside from the soft rustle of pine needles in an infrequent breeze.

Ten minutes later he walked back to the stone house. Sebastien was sitting on a tree stump. Johnny Boy went in the house, drank a full glass of water, filled two, and carried them outside. They sat and drank. The glare of sun shone behind Sebastien, sending his shadow across the dirt to end a few inches in front of Johnny Boy's boots. It was coincidence, not design, but Johnny Boy saw the potential significance in everything. His mind aflame with questions, he remained quiet, facing the small, placid man who was as contained and patient as an apex predator. The man rarely blinked. He finished the water and held the glass loosely on his thigh as if prepared to use it as a weapon.

"Sebastien," Johnny Boy said.

The man nodded.

"I'm John Tolliver Junior. They called me Johnny Boy at home because my dad had the same name. You can call me John."

"Jean," the man said, pronouncing it in the French way.

"Jean," Johnny Boy said.

He repeated it to himself, duplicating the accent, his name now beginning with a "zh" sound like the Hungarian actress Zsa Zsa Gabor. He knew the name vaguely due to her sister Eva, who'd starred in a rural television show called

Green Acres. Johnny Boy had loved the reruns as a kid. The theme song appeared in his head and he began whistling it, a spontaneous response to his own churning thoughts. Sebastien tipped his head half an inch like a curious dog at the sound.

"I like to talk," Johnny Boy said. "Do you?"

Sebastien shook his head once to indicate no.

"Well, I'll do the talking for both of us, then. I don't know where I am exactly. But maybe it doesn't matter now."

Again Sebastien moved nothing except his head, this time only a half shake, a brief no.

"Did Mick tell you why I'm here?"

Sebastien held his gaze steady on Johnny Boy as if debating the question or how to answer. He'd met Americans before, mostly soldiers, diplomats, clandestine operatives, and the occasional self-important businessman. This particular American was none of those. Mick had placed Tolliver here for safekeeping, saying only that he needed time to heal up inside from having committed violence. Sebastien understood. It was the reason why Sebastien had renounced his British citizenship and relocated to Corsica. Here he had no history, no enemies. It was as close to a fresh start as a man with his past could have.

The few Corsicans with whom Sebastien had formed cordial relationships were relieved that he was not from mainland France. He was known in the nearest village as a solitary man with no interest in politics, women, or the growth of clementines and almonds. He was always polite, extremely alert. Some people concluded that he was a writer or recovering from the sorrow of heartbreak. Others believed him to be a ne'er-do-well heir to a prominent foreign family who financed his exile to prevent their own embarrassment. Sebastien neither encouraged nor discouraged the oblique inquiries along these lines.

The village offered a small café that billed itself as a brasserie, though it had none of the traditional formality. A single meal was served, different each day. Small, round tables and spindly chairs. A four-foot bar for beer, gin, whiskey, and espresso. Sebastien had gradually befriended the proprietor with a soft approach as if he was a target for an operation. Titus was a big man with long hair, proud of his heritage, who spoke French, old Corse, and a rough Italian. Sebastien alluded to past problems with his ex-wife's family. He eventually paid Titus a monthly amount to immediately dispatch a young man with a message if a stranger asked questions about Sebastien. Titus agreed immediately. A lifelong romantic with his own history of fraught love affairs, he was unmarried but had two children by different women, whom he dutifully supported. Always in need of money, Titus knew how to keep a secret. They shook hands on the agreement.

Now Sebastien sat on the stump looking at this scrawny American, who was clearly suffering from emotional duress. There were dozens of psychological phrases that came down to the same thing—he was anxious and depressed, bereft as a bird in a storm unable to find its destroyed nest. Mick

had saved Sebastien's life many years ago, a debt impossible
to repay. Looking after this man was part of it.

He watched Johnny Boy—Jean—struggle to manu-
facture a verbal sentence.

"What do I do?" Johnny Boy said.

"Do?"

Encouraged by the single word, Johnny Boy spoke
faster with rising excitement.

"Yes, do," he said. "I have to do something. Anything.
There's nothing to read and I can't just sit, walk, and sleep. I
like to stay busy. I like to organize things, especially papers
and books. I can't stop thinking. I need to look at my hands
and see them do something. What do I do?"

Sebastien gave a slight nod, stood, placed the empty
glass on the stump, and walked away. His tread made little
sound. Dust seemingly refused to rise as he lifted each foot.
He vanished around the bend.

Johnny Boy sat immobile in blindsided shock. A few
weeks ago he'd had a home, a job, and a future. Now he
was alone in a strange country, watching the air where
Sebastien had been. He didn't know how to proceed, could
barely feed himself. He'd heard of denial, read about it, but
had never been able to fully comprehend it. How could one
deny what was obvious and clear to all, including oneself?
Now he understood. None of this could be real. It was
impossible to accept.

Unknown scents floated on the air from the ground
cover. A few trees he recognized—pine, juniper, and maybe

a variation of laurel. He wondered if he was homesick. He'd never lived anywhere but one county in Kentucky, had never yearned for travel or wider connections. He didn't miss it, not yet, which perplexed him. Perhaps he could consider this a vacation in a lonesome spot, the first place he'd ever visited, and nearly as beautiful as the hills of home. He wondered how far the ocean was, in which direction it lay.

He drank another glass of water, then carried both inside and washed them. Standing at the metal sink, he pushed aside the translucent curtains, wondering how he'd get through the rest of the day, then the night and tomorrow, all the days that lay ahead like a long ribbon of uncertainty. He was in a foreign land. He'd always be here. He'd lost everything. He could think of nothing other than himself. His mind ran swift as a rain gully after a storm, but instead of flowing into a creek, the water circled back and fed itself. Each cycle picked up velocity and deepened the rut. His future had been snatched away without warning. He struggled by the minute to prevent strangling on his thoughts and feelings.

The clatter of rattling rock made its way through the quiet of thick stone. He peered through the limited sight lines of the window, then went outside. A hog casually browsed the underbrush, heading downhill as if bound for a fixed destination. It was dark black, a color Johnny Boy had never seen on a hog, smaller than those from home. It must have escaped from a farmer's pen.

"Hidy, hog," he said.

The hog glanced at him as if in vague acknowledgment of a fellow mammal, then continued its snuffling of the land. Even a hog had work, Johnny Boy thought, but not me.

"Where you headed?" Johnny Boy said.

The hog ignored him, slowly wending its way downhill. I'm talking to a damn hog, Johnny Boy thought. He recalled hearing about an old-time monk who preached to birds and conversed with animals, including fish. He later became a saint. Maybe Johnny Boy was undergoing a religious experience and would become a mystic. The hog stepped behind a boulder, suddenly gone, and Johnny Boy considered the idea that he was hallucinating. Maybe he was home in bed with a terrible fever dream or in a coma. He'd recover with an amazing story to tell. It was a preposterous notion that he didn't believe. Sebastien had vanished, now the hog had, too. He himself had vanished just as abruptly from home.

He heard a different sound, steadier and continuous with intermittent rattles. Turning to it, he expected to see another hog or a few young ones seeking their mother. Instead it was Sebastien pushing a wooden wheelbarrow, gripping the handles tightly, his posture leaning back to prevent it from getting away. His cargo consisted of a long-handled spade, a mattock, a metal rod, a small sledgehammer, and a rake. Nestled beneath was a canvas hat with a wide, floppy brim. Johnny Boy wondered if this was a further hallucination.

"Did you see that loose hog?" Johnny Boy said. "It was blacker than a cow's insides."

"They live here."

"Where?"

Sebastien spread his arms to indicate the entire mountainside, then shrugged slightly as if saying, where else? Johnny Boy didn't understand. In fact, he realized, he didn't understand anything anymore. Comprehension wouldn't alter the circumstances. He was alone in a lonely place facing a stranger.

"What do you want me to do?" he said.

"Clear the land."

"What land?"

"Start where you stand."

Johnny Boy stepped back to study the earth below his feet. When he lifted his head, Sebastien had already silently begun his departure, was nearly out of sight, his shadow dwindling, then gone. Hogs live here, Johnny Boy thought. They wander around, wild but not unfriendly. So do I.

He picked up the shovel and stabbed the dirt where he'd stood. The hard ground resisted and he pressed his boot to the kickplate, then stomped until the blade gained two inches of purchase. He worked an hour, sweating heavily in the sun, then remembered the hat. Originally light blue, the color had faded to gray and white, the brim stained from another person's dirty hands. He drank water and switched to the mattock as a means to loosen the resilient dirt. By evening he admired a six-by-six-foot section of cleared land, barely two inches deep.

That night he slept well, his mind stilled from labor. He awoke with aches throughout his muscles but returned to work, stopping only for water and food. His appetite was returning. With greater alertness and energy, his mind replayed his final hours in Kentucky. What should he have done before events went too far? He had no idea. It was too late. He was stuck trying to figure out how to accept the consequences. He continued to dig the hard earth, focusing on the shovel and dirt.

Chapter Nine

On the road to town, Mick radioed dispatch that he was changing location, and asked after Raymond.

"Deputy Ray-Ray," Sandra said. "Never thought I'd say that."

"Try Deputy Kissick, then."

"That's even worse. He's still on that barn call. Where you headed?"

"Jailhouse. Need to talk to Zack Jones."

"Uh-huh," she said. "I see."

He ended the call, thinking about the empty safe at Ajax. His impulse was to visit his sister but he recognized that dropping by the Kissick house was merely another means to avoid talking to Jones.

The new jail was a few years old, double the size of the old one, and already packed with inmates. Just as a goldfish would grow to the size of its container, a jail would soon fill to capacity. He parked in the area for official visitors, identified himself, and showed his badge. While waiting, he recalled the last time he'd interviewed a suspect here. Mick had been a civilian with special privileges helping his sister with her first homicide case. The suspect's alibi was intact enough to be released. A few days later he was murdered.

Mick left his gun and badge with a guard, stepped through a full-body scanner, and went to a small interrogation room universally known as "the box" due to its low ceiling and lack of windows. Zack Jones was already there, sitting at a metal table bolted to the floor, his hands cuffed to a ring welded to the surface. Mick asked the guard to unlock his hands. The guard gave a grimace of disapproval, released the cuffs, and left. Jones rubbed his wrists, eyes downcast.

Mick had never seen him before and was slightly surprised by his appearance—soft and skinny with a small potbelly. His skin had the unhealthy pallor of someone who ate fast food, worked indoors under fluorescent lights, and was exposed to cigarette smoke. Dark eyes, bushy brows, and narrow shoulders. He didn't look like a killer but he didn't look like a ladies' man, either. Jones was one more miserable inmate—scared, sleep-deprived, and disoriented by the sudden change in his life.

"Do you know who I am?" Mick said.

Jones nodded, blinking like someone who needed glasses.

"I'm here for Peggy," Mick said. "Not you. Understand?"

Jones nodded rapidly. He lifted his eyes and Mick saw a glimmer of hope, the ancient delusion of potential reprieve. He would take what help he could get from any quarter.

"Where were you two nights ago?" Mick said.

"Ajax. Played a show."

"And after the show. Tell me what happened."

Jones shrugged and glanced away, then focused on his hands lying on the table side by side. His fingers were long in the way of a musician or a sniper. Mick wondered why Jones was being evasive—guilt, fear, or general discomfort. He could also be formulating a response he considered appropriate to the situation or one he thought Mick wanted to hear. It was clear that he was hiding something.

"If you want out of here," Mick said, "you need to talk to me."

"Why you?"

"Peggy asked me to. The cops think you did it. They can detain you for another twelve hours, then charge you. You had means, motivation, and opportunity. They're looking for the murder weapon."

Jones lifted his head and looked Mick straight on for the first time.

"I didn't do it," he said.

Mick nodded. There it was—the thing every incarcerated person always said regardless of guilt. They lied to cops, lied to themselves, or both simultaneously. Sometimes they told the truth. Mick studied his face carefully, instinctively taking in micro expressions. Jones's pupils had not dilated. There was no fresh tension along the jaw or forehead. He could be an excellent liar or telling the truth. Regardless, there was more that he wasn't saying, maybe because he was facing his wife's ex-husband.

Mick wanted to walk away and join Raymond in his investigation of the barn intruder. He suddenly wished he'd never retired from the army. It was a mistake, premature, motivated by temporary irritation that would have passed with time.

"According to multiple witnesses," Mick said, "you had an argument with Skeeter over money."

"He wasn't paying us right."

"I don't know what that means exactly."

"We're supposed to get the door, you know, the money from the cover charge. I'd say ninety people were there, maybe a hundred. That's like two fifty to three hundred bucks. He gave us one forty. Less than half. So yeah, I hollered at him about it."

"Sticking up for yourself."

"Yeah, and the guys, too."

"Had Skeeter ever shorted you before?"

"I don't know. Maybe. The other night it was real obvious."

"What'd he say?"

"Said that was all the money he took in. Said I couldn't see good enough past the end of the stage to know the crowd size. Said I was concentrating on playing. Said maybe I'd had too many beers to count."

"Had you?"

"I drank four beers total. One before each set. Then one afterwards. It's how I always do it. Keeps me loose, you know. But I don't get drunk because I got to drive home and sometimes work the next day."

"Still at Lowe's in Owingsville?"

"Yeah. If they're shorthanded they call me. I can't risk being hungover."

"Smart," Mick said. "Responsible."

He watched Jones's posture rise from the compliment. Mick wondered how rare it was for him to hear praise or if it meant more coming from Mick.

"I wouldn't shoot anybody," Jones said. "Especially not over a hundred and fifty fucking dollars."

"Somebody did," Mick said. "Somebody made Skeeter open up his safe and killed him. The town police think it was you."

"It wasn't."

"The judge will side with the cops. It's on you to disprove them."

"How?" Jones said.

"You need to account for your time when Skeeter got shot."

"I went home."

"What time?"

Jones's eyes momentarily shifted upward and to the left, and Mick understood he was dissembling. A lie was coming.

"I don't remember," Jones said. "Late. Peggy will know."

"She told the city police she was asleep and didn't wake up. She doesn't know when you got in."

Jones slumped toward the table, head down.

"That makes it your word against the cops," Mick said. "You know how that'll go."

Jones lifted his face to Mick, who could see the desperation stamped into his expression as if by a machine. It wasn't the face of a murderer but of a man feeling guilty about something else, something personal, something he didn't want anyone to know. Abruptly, Mick knew what it was.

Mick went to the door and knocked twice. The guard opened it.

"Be back in a minute," Mick said. "Keep him in here."

The guard grunted and re-cuffed Jones to the ring in the table. Mick walked down the hall to the main door and found a micro market used by staff and police officers. It was especially handy for drivers who'd transported prisoners long distances with no meal breaks. Mick got a bottle of water, a Coke, some kind of energy bar, and a Hostess cupcake. He used his credit card to pay and realized that he was buying food for the man who'd had an affair with his wife. Thinking that way was no good and would only lead to resentment or a decision based on emotion. He tucked it away. Jones was a suspect and it was Mick's job to find out what he knew.

Back in the cell, the guard uncuffed Jones, who stared at the food, then at Mick. He had a puppy dog quality with eyebrows that rose a little in the center of his forehead as if always seeking a friendly face. The kind of dog who'd hang around a family house until they fed him.

"You hungry?" Mick said.

"Yeah. Food in here's shit."

"You want out?" Mick said.

"Yeah. I want out."

Mick slid the bottle of water across the table. In his eagerness, Jones fumbled with breaking the seal on the plastic lid. He managed to get it open and drank half, sighed, and drank a little more. He capped it slowly and looked at Mick with a perplexed expression.

"Why'd you give me this?"

"It's what I did in Afghanistan. Everybody needs water there. Same in here. No good getting dehydrated in the desert. Or in jail."

Mick moved his hand closer to the food.

"Some guys in my position," he said, "they just go hard all at once. Threats and violence. My way is what I call the soft approach. It's like the carrot or stick. That water is the first carrot."

"I don't see a stick."

"Leaving you to rot in here is all the stick I need."

"Did that work in Afghanistan?"

"No. They were battle-hardened soldiers or fanatics. I don't think you're either one. And I don't think you killed Skeeter."

"I never."

"I think you were somewhere else that night. Not the bar and not at home. I think you don't want to tell me where."

Jones blinked rapidly, then looked away, glancing about like someone seeking misplaced keys. There was nothing but a concrete floor and gray walls. Mick knew he'd hit an open wound. He moved the energy bar, cupcake, and can of Coke in front of his hands as if prepared to push them across the table. The motion caught the attention of Jones, who stared at the food, then briefly at Mick, and back at the table.

"Couple things," Mick said. "You need to look at me first."

As if with great effort Jones shifted his vision to Mick, who nodded. Mick focused his left eye on Jones's left eye, a technique to reinforce nonaggression. Two angry people preparing for conflict stared hard at each other's right eye. Mick was trying to ease Jones into communication with the opposite approach.

"I don't care about Skeeter," Mick said. "I don't care who killed him. I don't care about you or the law. You hearing me?"

Jones nodded.

"What I do care about," Mick said, "is stopping anybody else from getting killed. You know how it is. Somebody will take a run at whoever killed Skeeter. That kind of thing keeps on going. Right?"

Jones nodded again.

"The cops think you did it," Mick said. "That'll get around the county if it already ain't. Makes you a target. In here, outside, at trial, in prison. Won't matter where. Family's family and that's all that matters in these hills."

A grim expression fastened onto Jones's face. He was a town guy but understood the ramifications. Mick could see the anxiety spread like a layer of sediment over what he already felt.

"I'm trying to help you," Mick said.

"Why would you?"

"I don't know," Mick said. "I been asking myself the same thing all day."

"This your way of trying to get her back?"

Mick thought it over briefly. For the first time Jones had impressed him by displaying some backbone.

"No," Mick said. "We're done. She's with you and y'all have two kids. She came to the station yesterday. First time we talked in a couple of years. She doesn't think you did it."

"I didn't."

"I believe you."

"I ain't for sure I want your help."

"I don't blame you," Mick said. "But right now they ain't nobody else. You'll get a lawyer, public defender probably, some kid fresh out of law school. This case won't look good in court. All manner of stuff will get dragged up—alcohol and weed habits, that DUI, getting a married woman pregnant, your work history. Then getting mad at Skeeter in front of witnesses two hours before he's murdered at the same place."

"I didn't do it."

"You still hungry?"

"Yeah."

"Tell me where you were and this food is yours. That's the last carrot."

Jones leaned back, stretching his back and neck, tipping his head toward the wall behind him. His breath was noisy, the air straining through his slightly pinched windpipe. Mick pitched his voice slightly higher, using a gentle tone.

"I won't say nothing to Peggy. You have my word on that."

Jones leaned forward again. For the first time he looked full on at Mick as if trying to comprehend the conversation.

"I don't understand you, man," Jones said.

"Sometimes I don't either. My own sister doesn't. Wherever you were, you can tell me or the town cops. They'll interview whoever your alibi is. Police car, uniform, maybe the lights. Hard to predict. But people will talk. Make their own story up and spread it around. You know what I mean."

Jones nodded.

"Me, I'm discreet," Mick said. "I'll check it out on the sly. If it's legit, I'll let Chief Logan know. He'll kick you loose. Your secret is safe. And so is whoever you're trying to protect."

"How do you know I am?"

"I'm good at figuring things out. What's her name, Zack?"

Mick had used Jones's first name deliberately, saving it till now. It was worth more than the lousy snacks on the table.

"Patricia Holloway," Zack said.

Mick pushed the food across the table, stood, and knocked on the door. The guard opened it immediately.

"I'm done," Mick said to him. "Do me a favor and let him eat that before you take him to his cell. I'll let Chet know you were cooperative."

The guard made a face of disgust and nodded.

Chapter Ten

At Linda's house Mick removed his sheriff's uniform and carefully placed it on a hanger in the closet. He'd gotten weary of uniforms in the army and had conceded to this one simply because he was the new sheriff. As he changed, he realized he'd been waiting for a reason to wear civilian clothes again. He put on a T-shirt and blue jeans with just enough fade not to look brand new, and a medium-width belt. He clipped his badge above his left pocket and a handcuff case behind it. On the right side he strapped a quick-release polymer holster for his Beretta M9 and put on a pliable cotton work shirt with long tails that would hide the gun and badge. On his feet he wore the same style of side-zip tactical boots that had gotten him through combat. For the first time in several weeks, he felt comfortable as he drove to the station.

Sandra was behind her desk on the phone as usual. She nodded vigorously to the person on the other end of the line. Mick could hear the rapid, tinny voice of the caller but couldn't understand the words. Every so often Sandra spoke, trying to end the call.

"Yes, ma'am," she said. "Yes, I understand. Yes, I'll tell the sheriff. Yes, ma'am, I promise. All right. Yes, ma'am. Thank you. Okay. Goodbye."

She hung up the phone, gasped, and rolled her eyes so hard they'd have snapped out of the sockets if not tethered. "Good golly," she said. "That was Mrs. Goodlett about the trespasser in her barn. Ray-Ray went out there. He said it was a deer. She didn't like that, thought he was making it up."

"A deer. Probably after food."

"He told her it wasn't a police matter. The barn needs repairs so the door will stay closed. She wants to see you personally. Says she knew your mama and Ray-Ray's mama and liked yours better. You going out there?"

"No, I trust Raymond. I need to do a little work here."

"Uh-huh," she said. "This your new uniform?"

"Yeah, I can blend in better."

"Good luck there," she said, and laughed.

Mick nodded, went to his office, and opened the computer. After ten minutes he learned that Patricia Holloway, thirty-eight years old, owned a house with her husband, and had a car registered in Eldridge County. No criminal record, not even a parking ticket. There had been no police calls to her address. A law-abiding woman born in Fleming County, she'd moved to Rocksalt and now lived six miles out of town on Sparks Branch.

Mick told Sandra he'd be back in an hour.

"What do I tell Ray-Ray?" she said.

"About what?"

"Well, let's see. How about his job?"

"Sit tight in case there's a call. He can use Johnny Boy's office. Tell him to read all open cases. There's only a few but he should know them. Then he can familiarize himself with recent arrests and any ongoing disputes."

"Ten-four, good buddy."

He left, frowning at her use of the ten code until he realized she was quoting an old song that romanticized long-haul truckers for their nomadic lives. In truth, those lives were fueled by amphetamines, and much of that generation had retired with poor health and bad backs. Many others died early. Now truck drivers were in short supply.

Mick drove out of town along Old Sixty, trying to refrain from thinking about what used to exist along the road. It had been widened, resurfaced, and painted with center stripes. Progress, he thought, represented by a continuous white line in the middle of the blacktop. A shoulder that extended two feet instead of six inches. Thinking this way wasn't necessarily bad but he knew it meant he was trying to avoid ruminating on his immediate task. He could potentially exonerate Jones with an alibi that might end his marriage. Maybe Peggy would return to Mick. He knew it was a case of false hope, like the condemned man mounting the scaffold and believing that the rope would break. They'd just hang him again. Getting back with Peggy would be the same thing. A familiar noose.

Sparks Branch was an older blacktop road named for the creek it followed up a wide holler. Every road in the hills meandered along the route of a waterway that swelled in spring, trickled in summer, and was often dry by August. Mick drove slowly past the Holloway house, which was set back from the road on higher ground. It was a small wood-frame house painted white with gray trim. Air-conditioning units protruded from two windows. A single car was parked in the driveway. He turned around, drove back to the house, and parked.

The grass had recently been mowed and the weeds trimmed around the maple in the front yard. A slim front porch was so narrow that it seemed like an afterthought tacked in place. One half was screened behind two flower bushes that flourished in the sun. Embedded in the ground below each bush were plastic feeders filled with syrupy liquid. A hummingbird circled one feeder, then cautiously approached as if taking midair steps an inch at a time. Another hummingbird swooped from the sky like a tiny green bullet. Briefly the two birds engaged in an aerial battle over feeding rights. Their fierce combat caused both to lose altitude until one flew rapidly away.

Mick climbed three steps to the slatted floor of the porch, walking with a heavy tread to announce his presence. He tapped at the door and took two steps back,

double-checking that his shirttail concealed the gun and
badge. With a benign expression, he waited. The front door
opened and a woman appeared behind the screen door.

"Mrs. Holloway?" Mick said.

"Yes, that's me. I don't believe I know you."

"I'm Jimmy Hardin's boy, Mick."

She nodded, trying to place him in her mind's catalog
of family names. He watched her rake through the Hardins
she knew but not quite land on his particular bunch.

"I'm from way on the other side of the county," he
said.

"I'm from Ewing, close to Flemingsburg."

"Pretty country. I'm hoping you can help me with
something, Mrs. Holloway."

"You can call me Patricia."

"Thanks, Patricia. I'm here about Zack Jones."

A sudden fear tightened her face like snugging a bow-
line knot.

"Are you a lawyer?"

"No, ma'am. He doesn't need one yet. I'm trying to
make sure he never does. The Rocksalt police have him in
jail about Skeeter."

"I heard," she said. "Poor Skeeter. I don't think Zack
did it."

"I don't either."

"What's this got to do with you?"

"Not much," Mick said. "It's a favor for the family. My
sister was the sheriff till she got hurt. I'm filling in for her."

"You don't look like a sheriff."

"I have to say, ma'am, I don't feel like one most of the time."

He pulled the tail of his shirt aside to reveal the badge clipped to his belt.

"I gave up on the uniform," he said. "And I'd rather drive my papaw's old truck than the county SUV."

He waited, giving her time to contemplate the fact that the county sheriff was standing on her porch. She clearly knew Zack but seemed puzzled as to why Mick was here.

"Patricia," he said, "can you and me talk a minute?"

"All right," she said. "It's already too hot for me out there."

She pushed the screen door open. He entered a room that was stunningly cold, the air vibrating with the air conditioner's fan that rattled from loose mounting screws on the motor. She adjusted a knob and the sound dropped by half. She straightened slowly as if her back was bothering her.

He closed the door behind him. The front room was neat and tidy with a couch, two chairs, and a coffee table topped by glass. A medium-size flat-screen television sat on another coffee table to which someone had fastened heavy casters for easy moving. It was angled toward the couch, the sound low. Two cowboys galloped across a barren landscape.

"I love *Gunsmoke*," she said. "Used to watch it with my mamaw after school."

She went to the far end of the couch, and eased down, using one hand on the armrest to support herself. Mick wondered how badly she was hurt, if Zack had done it, or maybe her husband. He sat in one of the chairs and slumped to lower his head below hers, while tucking the shirt over the Beretta. They watched the cowboys dismount in front of a ranch house.

"My papaw liked *Gunsmoke*," Mick said. "But we lived too far in the woods for good reception. Had an antenna outside mounted on a post. Wasn't worth a nickel."

"What about a dish?"

"Papaw said he wasn't about to pay for something that ugly."

He squeezed out a chuckle and she nodded.

"Reruns are on a lot," she said. "If you know the right channel. Now what's this all about?"

"I'm trying to get Zack out of jail. That means finding out where he was the night Skeeter got killed. Three nights ago. Zack played a gig at Ajax. After that, his whereabouts aren't exactly known."

"You're hunting an alibi," she said. "Like on *Dragnet*."

"Yes, ma'am, I am. Do you know where Zack was?"

"He was here."

"What time was that?"

"After midnight. Around twelve thirty. I'd already had four hours' sleep, like a nap, I reckon. Not too hard to wake up."

"How would you describe his frame of mind?"

"Pretty upset at first. Mad about Skeeter and money. But he calmed down and we had a long talk."

"Do you remember when he left?"

"About four thirty."

"He stayed that long?"

"Yeah, he took a rest on the couch. The beer caught up with him. Slept some, then left."

Mick nodded, thinking that Ajax was at least thirty minutes away. If Zack had gone back to the bar from here, Skeeter was already dead. Patricia could be lying but Mick didn't think so.

"It's none of my business," he said, "but I have to ask. Did Zack do anything while he was here?"

"Like what?"

"Maybe hurt you or something?"

"Are you kidding? Zack wouldn't swat a gnat. Thought too much of his fingers for playing guitar. He's gentle-turned. That's why I liked him."

"Do you think you could tell me what y'all talked about?"

"I'd just as soon not," she said. "Do I have to?"

"No, I'm not here officially. It's a town case and right now they think they got enough to charge him. I talked to Zack today. He said he was here. If he left when you said he did, that might put him in the clear. The police chief is an old buddy, Chet Logan. He'll listen to me. But he'll want to know a little more."

"Why's that?"

"Well, he's got a dead body is why. Zack didn't say word one about you to Chet. Just me. Nobody knows I'm here. I can talk to Chet and that way you won't have city cops at your door."

Patricia pushed herself to her feet.

"I'll be right back," she said. "I got to, you know."

She used a remote to increase the volume on the TV, then slowly walked down a short hall. Mick heard a door close behind her. The cowboys crouched behind a giant boulder, pinned down by gunfire. There were so many ricochets that it seemed as if the rock was the target. The habit of watching television had never fastened to Mick, which put him at a disadvantage when people talked about their shows, discussing actors as if they were personal friends. He supposed everybody on *Gunsmoke* was long dead. Television was a time capsule, maintaining the youth and beauty of people wearing costumes.

The front room had a low bookcase jammed with romance novels on two shelves. The surface held knick-knacks, including three sets of ceramic salt and pepper shakers—a pair of cheerful pigs, a bull and a matador, and a jolly elderly couple wearing spectacles. There were no family photographs, which was unusual for the hills. Three framed pictures hung on the walls, the paint-by-numbers kind, each with precise and unwavering brushwork.

Patricia returned and lowered the TV volume. Mick could hear a toilet tank refilling. With the same protective care as before, she placed herself on the couch and stared at him.

"Will I have to testify?" she said.

"No. If charges are dropped, that's the end of it."

"My husband works construction in Ashland. Makes good money and always goes for the overtime. He's away most of the time. He's gone now. He'll be home Wednesday with three days off, then back to Ashland. That means I'm alone a lot. Zack and I got mixed up together. Not that often but often enough, know what I mean?"

She patted her stomach and lifted her eyebrows in a knowing way.

"I told him to come over the other night," she said.

"You called him? Or texted? There was nothing on his cell phone."

"I called Ajax and asked the bartender to tell Zack that Rose called. Zack knew it meant to come by later. That way his wife and my husband couldn't accidentally find a text. Or on purpose if they were looking."

"I understand," Mick said. "Did he know about your, uh, situation."

"I told him the other night when he came over. Then I ended things with us."

"How'd he take it?"

"I think he was a little relieved. I don't want anything from him. My husband will think the baby's his and I'll thank you not to tell anyone different."

"I won't."

"What about your police chief buddy?"

"No ma'am, you got my word," Mick said.

"Can you get Zack out of jail?"

"I think so, yes. I believe you and Chet'll believe me. I'll keep it between me and him."

"If you're not going to tell anybody about the baby, why'd you want to know what we talked about?"

"I needed to find out if you were lying for him."

She nodded in a distracted way and stroked the loose blouse covering her stomach. Mick stood and went outside. Within the screened in section of the porch he saw a hummingbird with its long, slender beak protruding through a single hole in the mesh. It was trapped, trying unsuccessfully to remove itself by flying backward. Mick stepped into the screened area and gently pressed his forefinger against the tip of the hummingbird's beak. The bird's wings increased their desperate motion until it slid free of the screen and fell. Halfway to the ground it recovered and arced into the sky. Mick remembered his grandfather placing a sugar cube on his tongue, lips stretched wide, in an effort to lure a hummingbird to feed from his mouth. It never worked. Papaw tried again and again while young Mick watched in delight.

He went to his truck, drove around a bend, and pulled over on the shoulder. Patricia Holloway's information cascaded through his mind like a series of hammer blows, each releasing a long-buried anxiety. His chest felt as if it was sinking into itself, then swelling beyond the confines of the truck cab. He inhaled as deeply as possible but was unable to get sufficient oxygen to the bottom of his lungs. The terrible sensation of suffocation rippled along his limbs like electricity powered by sorrow. His hands throbbed from gripping the rigid steering wheel. Numb and unable to move, he understood that he was reliving the end of his marriage. A lonely married woman. Secrecy and deceit. A pregnancy. Loss and grief in every direction.

He tried to regain himself. You're sitting in your truck, he thought. That's the windshield. You can see the veined leaves of a maple tree. The sky is blue. The windshield glass needs cleaning.

Utilizing a ferocious effort he managed to lower one hand from the steering wheel and turn on the wipers. They squeaked across the dry windshield in a stuttering motion. His view was no better but he'd taken action. He turned them off and continued to breathe as deep and slow as he could. He lowered his head to the steering wheel and wondered when he'd lost the ability to cry. The urge was in him but he couldn't find the valve to release the tears.

He continued to re-feel the end of his marriage, the end of a future he'd counted on. Part of him would always love her. People thought hate was the opposite of love but those emotions were twins that came from the same place, like a stone in its socket of earth. The inverse of love was indifference. He wanted to be as indifferent to Peggy as the rock was to dirt. She'd tossed him aside like an old shirt no longer needed. He was discardable. He wanted to tell her about Zack but knew he wouldn't. Doing so would be a petty act of vengeance. He'd always maintained a sense of decency and honor, even through his own pain, and he refused to compromise that part of himself.

He forced his legs to step out of the truck, cross a field of high grass, climb a slight slope, and enter the woods. Walking without direction, he moved deeper into the welcoming trees. His passage hushed the birds briefly until they dismissed him as a threat and their combined song began again, braiding into a continuous and calming sound. The woods enclosed him with the gentle solace of green.

At a slight open spot he lay down on his back. Light fell through the canopy of leaves. Despite their proximity, adjacent trees never overlapped. None of their leaves touched, as if each tree recognized its neighbor's space. They didn't compete or encroach but remained side by side like two draft horses working together to ease the other's load. Mick wondered if he would ever have that as part of his life.

Chapter Eleven

Johnny Boy walked up the hill to the other stone house and stopped in the same spot where he'd stood before. He counted seconds, then minutes, in his head, and went back down the hill to wait. Sebastien arrived on foot shortly after. He nodded approval of the area cleared of rock and scrubby plants.

"I'm out of food," Johnny Boy said.

Sebastien turned away and headed up the hill. Johnny Boy expected him to return with groceries but he heard the Renault before it came into view. Sebastien parked on the road, gestured for Johnny Boy to get in the car, and drove at a sedate pace, leaving a faint dusty wake that swirled into the low brush.

Sebastien recognized the American's distraught air, usually the result of trauma and stress. Sebastien had experienced it himself more than once, had observed it many times in war zones, and knew the best cure was focused

labor to prevent the flow of circular thinking that made
you feel worse. Some people relived the terrible event daily
and entered their own nightmares, arming themselves and
shooting their loved ones. That didn't seem to be the case
with Jean. He wanted food, not alcohol, and he'd worked
the yard well. Jean appeared more bewildered than anything. He was about thirty, but a quality existed within him
of being much younger and much older simultaneously as
if life had left him both stunted and aged.

"Do you have French?" Sebastien said.

"A French what?"

"Can you talk it?"

"No."

"Any other language?"

"Never had no need. I lived my whole life in Eldridge
County, Kentucky. Went to Florida once. They talk English but it was too crowded to suit me. And hot."

Sebastien slowed the car to a stop in the middle of the
road. He pointed out the window to a low tree.

"*Arbousier*," he said.

He indicated a low plant with small, tight buds on
their way to blossom.

"*Bruyere*."

He inhaled deeply and gestured for Jean to do the
same.

"*Asphodele*."

Johnny Boy sniffed the fragrance, realizing he'd been
smelling it since his arrival, a sweet aroma. The only visible

flowers were two feet tall, blooming at the bottom of the spikey stalk.

"*Asphodele*," he said.

Sebastien nodded, ignoring the clumsy accent.

"*Votre premier cours de Francais*," he said. "Your first French lesson."

He lifted his foot from the clutch, pressed the gas pedal, and continued along the winding road. They descended to a wider road and entered a small village. There were few cars. Bicycles and mopeds were parked indiscriminately, unlocked as if abandoned. There were more motorcycles than anything. Sebastien eased the Renault into a thin slice of shade, cut the engine, and got out. He waved for Jean to join him.

"It's two and a half klicks to here," Sebastien said. "You can walk it."

"Klicks?"

"About a mile and a half."

Johnny Boy followed him slowly, strolling in the center of the narrow lanes that wove through the collection of stone and wood structures. He and Sebastien were like mapmakers getting the layout before putting pencil to paper. A few cats watched them. From an occasional window a human face appeared, like a sentry. An older woman waited at a corner for them to pass. A couple shared a cigarette in a doorway. Coming toward them was a man in his forties wearing a workman's smock. He and Sebastien stopped to exchange a few words, then went on.

"That was old Corse," said Sebastien.

"He didn't look that old."

"No, his name is Petru. If you need medicine, he can get it. Corse is the old language. Some people keep it alive. No one expects you to. French is good enough for a foreigner."

"But you talk old Corse," Johnny Boy said.

"I have many languages. One of my three gifts."

They reached the end of the village and returned through a brief maze of tight alleys. Back on the main thoroughfare they entered a building with four tables and a four-stool bar. At one of the small, round tables, an older man sipped from the tiniest cup Johnny Boy had ever seen. He placed it on an equally tiny saucer beside a baby's spoon.

A big man with a deep tan and long hair hurried out of a side room bearing the first smile Johnny Boy had seen in days. He rushed toward Sebastien as if to embrace him, then stopped short. They shook hands, one quick motion, and Sebastien took a half step back. They spoke rapidly in French. The sound washed over Johnny Boy like a quick downpour that dampened his clothes but didn't reach his skin.

Sebastien turned to him.

"I told Titus you're with me. You can eat here any time. When you need groceries, tell Titus and he'll assemble them for you. Don't worry about paying him. He has some English so keep things simple. Now tell him hello."

"Hidy, Titus," Johnny Boy said.

"*Bonjour, Jean. Ça va?*"

Sebastien translated for Johnny Boy.

"Just say 'sa-vaw.' It means you're doing all right. Give him your name."

"Sa-vaw," Johnny Boy said. "I'm Johnny Boy. Jean."

Titus presented another quick, broad smile, leaned to Johnny Boy, and kissed him twice on each cheek. Amused by the evident discombobulation on the American's face, his smile opened more. Johnny Boy wanted to wipe his face with his hand but was unsure of protocol and didn't want to offend the first person he met.

"*Je suis Titus,*" Titus said. "*Bienvenu dans mon café.*"

"Say 'mare-see,'" Sebastien said. "Don't hit the R too hard."

Johnny Boy did his best and Titus nodded encouragement. He and Sebastien spoke again in French. The old man at the table studiously ignored them, which Johnny Boy knew was an indication that he was paying scrupulous attention. Two younger men entered and stood at the bar as if prepared to linger for hours until Titus could attend to them. Sebastien addressed Johnny Boy.

"Titus will arrange for a friend to teach you French. You are to come here every day except Sunday. One to two is lunch. French lessons two to four."

"Okay."

"*D'accord,*" Sebastien said. "That means okay. 'Da-kore.'"

He spoke to Titus, who ushered Johnny Boy to a table and poured him a glass of water, leaving a full carafe behind.

The front door closed behind Sebastien before Johnny Boy realized he'd slipped away.

The café had high ceilings to accommodate the heat. A few items hung from the old walls, including a flag depicting a dark-skinned man wearing a white bandanna. No one acknowledged Johnny Boy, not even the slightest glance to confirm his existence. A severe sense of estrangement passed through his body. Was he really in another country, sitting at a rickety table in dim light? Was he really Johnny Boy Tolliver? He curled his fingers and touched them together. He could feel that. Water from the glass cooled the inside of his mouth. He was alive but felt separate from his body as if he could see himself in the world. Electricity seemed to run through his torso and limbs like he was holding tight to a low-voltage wire. He lifted his palms to see if his fingers were trembling from the current. They weren't moving. Maybe his eyes were shaking in tandem with his hands.

Time slid by inexorably and when Titus brought a large bowl, cloth napkin, and utensils, Johnny Boy had no idea if he'd sat five minutes or an hour. Maybe the French used a different clock the same way Sebastien measured distance in klicks, not miles. Titus placed the bowl with a flourish and casually dropped a chunk of bread on the table.

"*Bon appétit,*" he said. "*Civet de sanglier aux champignons.*"

"Thank you," Johnny Boy said. "Mare-see."

Titus nodded gravely, stepped backward slowly, and opened his arms in the universal gesture that meant "of course." The porcelain bowl contained thick soup with meat and dark mushrooms topped by chopped green leaves. His first bite was tentative, the fork composed of three tines on which he speared a morsel of meat and the tiniest mushroom. It was pork, rich as fresh venison, but not as tough. The flavor enveloped his mouth. He chewed longer than necessary. For the first time since leaving Kentucky, he had a sensation of joy, minor but nearly overpowering. He ate it all as slowly as possible. He'd never eaten for pleasure but always fast, sitting in his car, watching documentaries or reading history.

Now he could feel the food transforming to energy in his body. Using the bread to mop out the bowl, he drank the rest of the water. He tried to relax but the chair was not designed for reclining. The seat was as small as everything else in Corsica and he supposed big people spilled over the edges.

Titus's face held a sublime expression of approval as he removed the empty bowl, then returned with a tiny cup of black liquid on a saucer. He set it before Johnny Boy and adjusted the position for ease of handling. The crook of the handle was too small for his fingers, it was merely for holding between thumb and forefinger. Johnny Boy supposed that scarcity was part of life on an island. How, then, had Titus grown so big? Genetics. A diet of hog stew. Johnny Boy had little data, only speculation, which sent his mind reeling. Who was this generous man? How did he come to operate the only restaurant in the village? Why did he have long hair? What was between him and Sebastien?

The miniature cup was hot and he let it cool before sipping it, copying the method of the old man, who had relit a hand-rolled cigarette. It was coffee, the strongest Johnny Boy had ever ingested. The caffeine jolted through him. He finished it and immediately wanted another to perpetuate the tingling of his limbs and sudden alertness. He'd felt similarly the first time he drank whiskey, which was why he never drank it again. For no reason he could name, he wished he smoked, a habit he'd never had. He sat in wonder at the odd transformation of his own mind and body, remaining immobile for an indeterminate period. Though he'd never parachuted, he felt as if his body was in free fall and he was watching himself drop through the air. When he landed, he'd run and never stop.

The front door opened and a slice of sunlight widened as it crossed the tile floor, darkened by a shadow of someone entering. Sebastien walked to the table. Titus joined them and the two spoke fast, the tones guttural. Titus laughed as if hearing a favorite joke he'd forgotten years back.

"Let's go," Sebastien said. "*On y va.*"

"What about the bill?" Johnny Boy said.

Sebastien shook his head and headed to the door. Johnny Boy stood to follow, escorted by Titus.

"*A demain,*" Titus said.

They stepped into the sudden sun, the angle of dark and shadow in the street sharp as a blade. Johnny Boy blinked and stared into the shade so his pupils could constrict. They walked to the Renault. In the back seat was a box with canned food, powdered milk, coffee, potatoes, nuts, cheese, and a chunk of ham. Sebastien drove slowly out of the village along the route they'd come. Johnny Boy memorized the turns, difficult because the terrain was all scrub and rock. As if reading his mind, Sebastien spoke.

"Maquis. It's called maquis. The growth."

"I have some money," Johnny Boy said. "Mick gave me some and he owes me more. Who do I pay? You or Titus?"

"Don't worry about it."

"Owing somebody doesn't sit right with me."

"Hawala."

"What?"

"A way to transfer money without the money actually moving."

"Like banks?"

"No. Banks leave a trail. Hawala uses middlemen and passwords."

"Nobody steals it along the way?" Johnny Boy said.

"There's nothing to steal. It's a very old system based on honor and trust. I'll receive money from Mick eventually. It's not fast. Might go through a few people and countries. Word of mouth is slow. But it'll get to me, then to you in cash. No record. Nobody can trace the money to find you. No paper trail or electronic trail. Nothing to link anyone along the way."

"Who uses it?"

"Money launderers. Terrorists. Aid workers in Africa. Spooks all over."

Johnny Boy wanted to ask what kind of ghost needed money. Hawala was one more thing he didn't understand, along with the language, the strolling hog, and the sky's deep hue. Nothing made sense. He wondered if it ever would. His previously well-tended life had become bewilderingly strange overnight. He could barely recall who he was, where he came from. He was forming a new sense of himself by the moment.

"How do you know Mick?" he said.

Sebastien didn't answer. Johnny Boy got out at his house and carried the crate of provisions inside, hearing the crunch of rubber on rock as the Renault trundled away along the hard-packed road. The familiarity of the sound offered Johnny Boy a slight comfort.

For the next several weeks Johnny Boy's life settled into a pattern that he began clinging to for stability. In bed by nine, asleep by ten. Up at six o'clock to work outside, then explore the terrain in an incrementally widening circle around the dwelling. He rested when necessary, ate at regular times, and drank four liters of water per day. Concerned that he might lose his wallet in the maquis, he quit carrying it. It made no difference to his life. He had no need for money or identification. He was still Johnny Boy Tolliver but nobody cared. In Corsica he was Jean or *l'Americain*. In the absence of a phone or a clock, he used the sun's position as a guide for the walk to Titus's café, where he ate and received his daily lesson in French.

His tutor was a woman of indeterminate age—thirty-five to sixty—who'd learned English while working for a small publisher in London. Madame Moncoso's hair was a startling silver as if she'd given up trying to color it dark and instead went the other way, letting it run bright as flatware. Sometimes it was plaited in mysterious tucking folds. Or it was held back by small, sparkling clips. When she talked he watched her mouth to learn how she formulated words, the accent emanating from the depth of her throat. He never remembered what color her eyes were. Nevertheless, within two weeks he'd developed a schoolboy crush on her. She offered him a kind of female attention he'd always lacked. His experience with romance was limited to one girlfriend a few years ago and half a dozen cases of unvoiced, obsessive devotion.

Wanting to impress Madame Moncoso, he worked hard on his French, which improved by the week. She was always in the café when he arrived, steadfast in her seat, posture erect, sitting before blank paper, fresh pencils, and workbooks. To widen his vocabulary she gave him a small English–French dictionary, a gift he cherished by granting it a special spot in the dark stone house. She never spoke personally and he made no inquiries about her. They'd begun with nouns in sight—table, window, floor. Cutlery and dishware. A few basic phrases of introduction, please and thank you, and the crucial "I would like to have . . ."

After an overview in English about the difference in formal and informal use of "you," she dismissed the formal as being unnecessary on the island. *Pas necessaire.* From there they progressed to present- and past-tense verbs. With nothing else to do but dig dirt, he practiced French the rest of his waking hours. She gave him assignments: Go to the pharmacy and ask for a specific item. Visit the mechanic about replacing a car door. Talk to a carpenter who performed roof repairs. Approach a stranger and ask if they'd seen a white cat.

All of these interactions transpired easily as if the people were willing participants in his education, the entire village a classroom. They were patient and polite, with an initial distance that gradually dwindled. No one expected him to follow through with a purchase or seek a lost pet. After six weeks he could make his statements and questions understood. However, he was only able to comprehend less than half of what others said. He relied on two phrases: *parlez plus lentement, si vous plait* and *je ne comprends pas.* "Please speak slowly" and "I don't understand."

At each afternoon's end, Madame Moncoso gathered her material and departed. There followed another half hour of French practice with Titus, who pointed out minor errors and suggested tips on pronunciation. Titus enjoyed using his English, often veering into a fractured conversation with Johnny Boy struggling with his terrible French and Titus his simple English. Titus's favorite phrase was "It's complicated." Johnny Boy interpreted that to mean that Titus had exhausted his reservoir of language and rather than admitting it, he preferred to claim the subject itself was too complex to explain. Regardless, they both enjoyed themselves. Each day Titus offered beer or espresso despite Johnny Boy's polite decline of either. The espresso jangled his fragile nerves and he didn't want to cloud his thinking with alcohol.

He became a familiar sight in the village. People nodded to him or if they passed nearby would greet him in French or Italian, sometimes in what he assumed was old Corse. Neither Titus nor Madame Moncoso ever mentioned Sebastien so Johnny Boy asked nothing about him. It was enough that everyone knew he was under Sebastien's care. He reminded himself daily that nothing mattered except improving his skill at communication and clearing the yard of rock.

Johnny Boy felt as if he was living in a dreamlike state, paying attention to the sun and little else. If people struggled against quicksand, they sank deeper. In a desert sandstorm you had to keep moving or be covered until suffocation. Both were counterintuitive, the way his own life was progressing now. He'd relied on order and routine, the precision of placing objects in the correct place—files at work, shirts hung in a certain order, books alphabetized on shelves. The money in his wallet was sequenced by value with each bill facing the same way. Now his patterns had shrunk to labor, food, walking, sleep, and learning French.

He walked up the road and stood for two minutes facing Sebastien's house, then returned. Very shortly afterward,

Sebastien arrived on foot. Johnny Boy asked for something
to read and Sebastien brought several novels from the nine-
teenth century. A daily reader, Johnny Boy had consumed
only nonfiction before. Now he read by lantern books that
Alexandre Dumas had written in the light of candles. During the day he studied handbooks to the local flora and
fauna in English and French.

He often had rough sleep—awaking from bad dreams
with his heart beating wildly and hard. His chest felt like
a wooden cask that someone was striking with a hammer.
He lay in bed, panting and terrified. He suspected it was a
combination of guilt and anxiety over his reason for fleeing
Kentucky. In the darkness he'd be unsure where he was.
He'd reach across the narrow bed to touch the cold stone
wall for comfort, a tactile reminder that he was alive.

Johnny Boy lost all track of time save day and night.
His extreme level of discomfort began to fade. He was
closer to connecting with himself, but understood it was a
different self from before. At times he couldn't sleep. Those
nights he lay awake thinking of home. He didn't miss particular people but yearned for the landscape, sounds, and
smells. He'd had satisfying routines, a way of being in the
world, the status of a minor law-enforcement officer. He
didn't know if he'd ever return or if he ever could. He'd
killed a man. Nobody knew it but Mick and him.

Chapter Twelve

After Linda's daily workout, she'd rested on the couch beside Shifty, who was intently watching a commercial with no sound.

"Hey, Shifty," Linda said. "Your TV working okay?"

"Yeah, I mute the commercials and try to figure out what they're trying to get me to buy. Not as easy as it used to be."

"To make you buy something?"

"To know what they're selling. Sometimes it comes at the end and nothing you saw made sense."

"Like what?"

"Diabetes medicine. Car insurance. All manner of stuff."

The commercial ended and Shifty used the remote to raise the volume to a piercing roar that ended the conversation. Linda's doctor had advised her to be positive but the only good thing to come from getting shot was having lost a little weight. First the trauma, then the terrible hospital food, followed by an emotional slump. Juan Carlos had placed her on Raymond's diet of protein and vegetables. For Shifty and himself he prepared richer meals. Or he had until Raymond left. Now he drifted morosely around the house. Two days ago Juan Carlos had hired a prep cook, a young man who talked too much, to fulfill Raymond's job. Albin had been a cab driver and weekend stock car driver until he was involved in a crash at the track and couldn't drive for a while. His steady chatter was the reason Shifty kept the volume high on her TV.

Twice a week Linda drove to the hospital for rehabilitation required by the county because she'd been hurt on the job. Throughout the slow and painful process, Linda forewent pain medication aside from ibuprofen and naproxen. At Holbert's drugstore in Rocksalt the salesclerk always asked how she was coming along. The entire county knew her story. Church groups prayed for Linda. Strangers offered tips such as gathering silver moss under the dark of a new moon and applying it to her wound. Linda thanked everyone politely, knowing that she was ensuring her reelection in a few years. A woman who returned to the job of sheriff after being shot in the line of duty could defeat any man who ran against her. She parked in the hospital lot and went to the physical therapy room.

Her rehab had recently expanded to include a "walking coach," a much younger woman with a perpetual cheer that was barely tolerable. Alice drove from Lexington to see patients twice a week. In a bright, lilting tone Alice explained that Linda instinctively protected her damaged leg, a habit that would confound her in the future. Alice studied Linda's gait as she made her way back and forth in ten-foot increments, going nowhere. It was worse than a treadmill. Despite Linda's misgivings, Alice's suggestions were helpful—lift your foot a little more, don't rock back and forth, keep your shoulders parallel. Move both arms smoothly at the same rate.

Today Alice nodded with the enthusiasm of a puppet with a loose head.

"Everything's great," Alice said. "You're walking like a champ!"

"It's still tight."

"That's normal. But not like before, right? You should start walking outside now. Quarter mile first, then three-quarters of a mile. Try to get to a full mile in a couple of weeks. Step it up when you're ready."

"All right."

"You don't need to come in here anymore."

"I'd like to keep doing it," Linda said. "It's good for me to get out. Good discipline, too."

Alice's face clouded over, tautening with fear. She leaned close, her voice quiet and serious, the professional optimism eradicated from her tone.

"You really shouldn't," she said. "I'm giving you a full release. It's for the best."

"Is this some insurance thing?" Linda said. "Everything's covered by the county."

"No, it's not that. As soon as I sign off, you have one more week till you go back to work. Coming in here is not good for you now."

"What's going on?"

"That's all I can say. And I shouldn't be telling you."

"Are you in trouble?"

"No," Alice said. "You are. Don't come back."

Alice stepped back and smiled brightly as if in a dental advertisement, showing the crisp gleam of her small teeth.

"Your recovery is complete!" she said, her voice unnaturally loud.

She moved away and Linda noticed that her assistant was in the room, a young woman in floral scrubs, intent on the flickering screen of a computer. Maybe Alice had spoken loudly for her benefit. The assistant left and Alice tapped a few keys swiftly. A printer began its asthmatic clatter and slowly produced three pages. Alice initialed the first two, signed the final page, and handed them to Linda. Her voice was low again, a faint whisper.

"Go," she said. "I don't have a choice."

Linda nodded and left, jarred by Alice's abrupt shift. She had behaved like a co-conspirator but Linda had no idea why. She'd seemed frightened, as if delivering a coded warning—but of what?

She went to the ER and asked for Dr. Bob, the physician who'd taken care of her during her long hospital stay. The receptionist said that he was with a patient but was due for a break soon. Linda sat in a corner and read the physical therapy discharge forms while she waited. It was official, dated today, granting Linda a clean bill of health, her leg healed. Perhaps Alice was quitting her job and didn't want the hospital administration to know. Every time someone walked by she looked up in case it was Dr. Bob.

Robert Fitzgerald had grown up in a mixed neighborhood of Philadelphia, son of a teacher's aide and a sailor in the merchant marine. He was the first in his family to attend college. During his sophomore year he quit and returned home to help care for his younger sister, who became sick from a rare illness. Her death shattered the family. Robert switched schools and committed to becoming a doctor. After his internship, he entered a program that would eliminate his medical school debt if he agreed to work in an area with a demonstrated shortage of health care professionals. He opted for the mountains of Appalachia and was sent to a hospital in Eldridge County. The accents were nearly unintelligible to him, as was his to the local people. He bridged part of the cultural gap by introducing himself as "Dr. Bob," a rare casualness for a doctor in the hills. On his days off he hiked alone, learning to love the peaceful landscape, which offered four solid seasons, none extreme. After his mandated commitment of service, he decided to stay, surprising himself more than anyone. He'd dated two nurses, undertakings that went nowhere. They parted amicably and he put in more hours at the hospital as an antidote to loneliness.

He received a message that he had a visitor and changed into fresh scrubs, discarding the bloody set he'd worn treating a patient with a chainsaw wound. The chain had come off and wrapped itself deeply into the man's arm. He'd arrived at the ER stoically carrying the chainsaw in his other hand, having driven himself with the tool on the passenger seat. Bob cleaned the wound, stitched up the worst gashes, and warned the man to stay out of the woods for a while, knowing he would ignore the advice.

Bob stepped into the waiting room, pleased to see Linda.

"Hey, Sheriff," he said in his standard clipped tone.

"Dr. Bob," Linda said.

She stood to show him she could and extended her hand. They shook briefly, both smiling.

"How's the leg?" he said.

"A little better every day, more or less."

"Good. Stay on it. Recovery is up to you."

She gestured to the double doors of the emergency room.

"Things okay in there?" she said.

"Yeah, yeah. Men get hurt in the woods every day. End of shift yesterday, a funny one. Guy came in with a hole in his palm. He was loading a flintlock rifle and accidentally shot the ramrod through his hand. Missed every bone. Had an old, dirty bandage on it. Said he would have come sooner but was in a marksmanship contest and stayed to shoot."

"I bet it was Pioneer Days over in Morgan County."

"Yup."

"How'd he do?"

"Took third. Said he'd a won if both hands worked. Tickled me no end. I got twenty minutes if nobody comes in. Use some coffee?"

She nodded and they went to the cafeteria, a small room with a steam table containing green beans, carrots, strips of fried chicken, and mashed potatoes. The woman behind the counter waved. Coffee was free for doctors and he poured two cups. They sat at a corner table. One wall held a display of black-and-white photographs of women on horseback, the early days of Frontier Nursing in the hills. The hospital founder and her nurse had delivered more than eight thousand babies in people's homes.

Linda liked Bob in a way that was unusual for her, which made her mistrust the feeling. She'd gone out with every available man in the town, then begun moving beyond its borders. The last few times she'd gone to a tavern out of the county, she'd concealed her occupation. It simplified the process of finding a man to go home with for the night. No one ever lived up to her long-term standards, which she knew was a white lie of self-deceit. Linda understood that she constantly sought reasons to end things with each man—the way he ate, how he dressed, even the car he drove. A man once swerved his truck to run over a snake sunning itself on the warm blacktop and she left the restaurant as soon as they arrived. She'd called a cab driven by Albin, paying him extra to take a different route, a long, looping series of roads, to avoid seeing the snake. Now she was living with Albin and facing a man across the table whose strange appeal made her uncomfortable. Worse, she had no job, no purpose, nothing to offer him but sex, and she liked him too much for that.

"Would you ever kill a snake?" she said. "Deliberately."

"Maybe if I was really hungry," Robert said.

She chuckled. His light brown eyes were flecked with green, visible at times when he moved his head, a quick glimpse of extra color. She watched for it, then felt awkward for doing so. Maybe it was natural to develop a bond with the person who'd healed you. He was probably accustomed to the situation, could see through it, knew how to extricate himself with delicacy.

"Do you know Alice?" she said. "The physical therapist from Lexington?"

"She consults sometimes. But I don't know her well. Hospitals aren't good for that. We work close enough. But then everybody goes back to their outside life."

"She acted funny with me today."

"Funny?"

"She released me from therapy," Linda said. "Pushed it on me, the papers, too. Like she was nervous about something. I didn't understand it."

"When you're done, you're done. She has other patients."

"I know, Bob. It was something else. Hard to explain."

"Her vibe?"

"I hate that word, but yes."

He grinned, his face transforming from the serious-
ness of a trauma doc to the expression of a child. Briefly she
saw the boy he'd been, the quick grasp of joy, his eyebrows
rising quizzically. She admonished herself for noticing his
eyes again.

"Could you please ask her about it?" Linda said.

"On one condition," he said.

They engaged in a mutual waiting period until he
noticed a nurse gesturing from the doorway, pointing to the
ER with a hurry-up motion. He stood, finished his coffee,
and set the cup down.

"I'll talk to Alice," he said. "Will you have supper with
me? Tonight? I get off work early."

He hurriedly scrawled his number on a prescription
sheet and placed it on the table.

"Text me," he said. "Okay?"

He gave her a quick nod to signal sincerity, then hurried away. Linda stared at the empty chair. For the first
time in months, she had an impulse to giggle, quickly sup-
pressed. She glanced about guiltily as if strangers might see
the surge of unexpected happiness or read her mind with
its carnal thoughts. What the fuck, she thought. I'm like a
damn schoolgirl. She left quickly without consideration of
her leg and drove to her own house.

She entered through the carport and into the kitchen,
pleased by the tidiness that her brother maintained in her
absence. She supposed it was his military background, the

years occupying small spaces with few possessions. The sink was clean, the dishes washed, the laundry folded. A stack of mail sat beside her mother's old bread box. No junk mail or advertising circulars, just bills and a few envelopes that appeared official in the new way that marketing departments had concocted to trick you into opening them. Linda was sloppy in general—didn't clean, sweep, mop, or close doors behind her. If she opened mail, she left the discarded envelope on the counter. More than a few bills got lost that way, each of which required a long phone call to eliminate the late charge and interest fee.

She was relieved to see the couch with a sheet and pillow for Raymond, which meant he wasn't sleeping in her bed. Mick used the room he'd had until age eight, when he began living with their grandfather in the cabin. Their mother had kept his bed and converted the rest of the space to a sewing room, then a storage chamber for her holiday decorations. Each carton was carefully labeled: Christmas, Easter, Halloween, Flag Day, Valentine's Day, V-E Day, birthdays for Lincoln, Washington, and Happy Chandler, former governor of Kentucky. The boxes were stacked in the corners. Linda didn't know why she'd kept them.

She texted Bob a single word—yes—then opened her bedroom closet, the sliding doors scraping in their metal track. For nearly a decade she'd planned on replacing them with a pair of double doors that swung outward. It was one of those small tasks she never got around to, reminding her of her mother's behavior. She cursed and kicked the closet in the precise spot to release the bent track's grip on the bottom of the door.

Linda found no clothes that appealed to her. She owned three dresses but wasn't about to wear one on a first date. She finally selected jeans reinforced with stretchy fabric, a pair of overpriced but striking cowboy boots from a trip to Nashville, and a flattering top. While picking through her closet, she wondered if she had a favorite color. No, she did not, then she wondered why not. Didn't most people? Well, so what, she sure as hell wasn't like most people, especially now, digging around in her mother's old house that was currently occupied by her brother and a Marine who'd never quite noticed he was out of the Corps. Maybe no Marine did.

Bob texted her back and they exchanged messages about where to eat. Neither of them wanted a restaurant in Rocksalt where they were likely to encounter people they'd met professionally. He'd either doctored them or she'd questioned them. Some she'd arrested. Small-town life meant there were few boundaries and a great deal of overlap—way too much most of the time. Bob suggested an Italian place in Maysville, an old river town with beautiful architecture from the late 1800s.

Linda napped and showered. Prior to Bob's arrival, she changed clothes four times and wound up with her original outfit. Her shoulder-length hair was usually pulled back in a tight clip for work. During her convalescence, a term she despised, she'd given her hair more freedom. Too much brushing and it hung limp. Too little and it frizzed out like a briar patch. It had grown to what she considered an awkward stage, but she doubted if anyone would notice or care. She didn't figure Bob had asked her on a date due to her straight brown hair. Maybe he liked split ends. Or maybe all he wanted was a break from the hospital.

She sat in the living room with the curtains parted to see Lyons Avenue. Linda had grown up with the same view, eagerly waiting to live on her own, which didn't last long enough. Most of the furnishings had belonged to her mother but Linda had added a smart TV and a new couch. Her mother's large mirror hung in the same spot with a faint horizontal line on one edge made by a permanent marker. It represented Linda's height. When the occasional suitor came calling, her mother positioned the young man at a specific spot on the rug to gauge his height, then reported to Linda whether she should wear heels or flats. It was a fond memory, one of the few she had of her mother. Linda hadn't worn heels in years, preferring fancy sneakers or boots.

A car trundled slowly up the street and eased into the driveway behind Linda's car. Bob got out, looked around as if double-checking the address, then headed for the front door. He was wearing a dress shirt, a belt, upscale jeans, and loafers. He knocked twice and she opened the door.

"Hey," she said. "First time I saw you in anything other than scrubs. Nice shirt."

"Thanks," he said. "You ready to go, or . . ."

She understood that he was giving her the opportunity to invite him in. She shook her head.

"My brother's staying here," she said. "With a friend."

"A special friend?"

"No," she laughed. "Nothing like that."

"Mick doesn't have his own place?"

"It's a long story. I'll tell you in the car."

They drove through town and took a state road through the hills, talking idly about the history of Maysville. As a newcomer, Bob was interested in the local area and knew far more than Linda did. To her, wealthy people lived in Maysville, descendants of the riverboat captains who built houses along the Ohio River. Bob drove past the Russell Theatre, built in the late 1920s.

"Art deco?" Linda said. "That's about it for what I know back then."

"Good guess, but no," Bob said. "It's a Spanish colonial style. You see it more in LA. Out there they call it Spanish–Moorish."

"It doesn't look real. Like a model or something. Made out of Legos."

"Or a movie set. The inside is amazing, too. Red and gold with turquoise trim. Fully renovated."

Linda nodded, thinking about the old movie theatre in Rocksalt. When it first opened the walls had stripes of flocked fabric, and if she scooted her feet on the carpet, then touched the wall, she'd see a spark from her fingertips.

Within three months the carpet became so clogged with dirt and grease that it would no longer conduct electricity.

"Do you like movies?" she said.

"Oh, you know. Yes and no. I go to the theatre for the big action pictures. But really, I'd rather stay home and watch on streaming. I can pause it when I want a snack or look up an actor on my phone. How about you?"

"Uh, I have trouble sitting still that long. Mainly I watch *Law & Order*. It's always on TV and if you miss something, you didn't really miss much. They just ruled out a few suspects while I was gone. Dun-dun!"

"I can't watch it if I see the opening credits. Whoever the big guest star is, that's the killer at the end. Kind of a spoiler, you know?"

"Yeah, like you telling me is, too."

She laughed to let him know it was a joke and they parked in the half-empty lot for Marinaro's Family Restaurant. It was an old-time red-sauce place with checkered tablecloths and murals of southern Italy on the walls. They ordered a glass of wine apiece, appetizers of pesto crostini, and pasta for the main course. Linda was surprised to find herself relaxing as she talked, dispensing with the standard self-conscious monitoring of her words that was habitual with most men, especially as the only female law-enforcement official in a six-county area. Bob didn't seem to care one way or another and she wondered if it was from working with female nurses. He talked of his childhood in Philadelphia and asked about her family. During a slight lull in conversation, she went with one of her standard questions—what's your favorite team?

"I grew up with the Steelers and the Phillies and the Sixers," he said. "No choice really. I loved sports as a kid. But after a while, it just seemed like grown men playing a children's game. All about money. Guess you're a Wildcat fan."

"I watched with my mother," Linda said. "She had special blue outfits when they were on TV. Half her clothes said 'Wildcat' on them somewhere. Then I got mad and quit watching when the rules changed."

"What do you mean?"

"Maybe it wasn't the rules but the referees. They stopped calling fouls and walking. Didn't seem right."

"Makes the game more exciting."

"I guess."

The waitress brought giant plates of pasta and they ate steadily, then rested. They skipped dessert and Bob had a cup of coffee for the drive back. Linda was dulled by the food and the gorgeous view of the night sky visible in the occasional patches of sky unencumbered by tree and hill. As a kid she'd walked to the top of a cemetery on a hill behind her house and lain on her back. The sky seemed to breathe from the twinkling. It was a pleasant memory, one she kept to herself. No telling how Bob might respond to a child lying down in a cemetery at night.

A few miles from Rocksalt she asked if he'd learned anything about the nurse's reason for pushing her to end her rehabilitation early. He was uncharacteristically silent for a while, then nodded in the dim light from the dashboard.

"Is that why you went with me tonight?" he said.

"At first, yeah. But I liked the food and conversation."

He drove into town, took the shortcut to Second Street, and turned onto Lyons Avenue. There were no streetlights, traffic, or pedestrians. Mick's truck stood in her driveway and the official sheriff's vehicle was parked on the street. A dim light shone through her mother's curtains. Bob eased to a stop, put the gear in neutral, and told her what he'd learned about Alice. Discharging Linda was not her idea but had come from her supervisor in Lexington. The boss had insisted without telling Alice why.

"You're welcome," he said. "Maybe we can have another meal sometime? Or, I don't know, take a hike, rent a boat at the lake. Something like that."

"Sounds good," she said. "I didn't mind it too much tonight."

"That sounds like a compliment."

"It was," she said. "Thank you for the night away."

She got out of the car and walked past Mick's truck into the carport. At the side door, she shot a quick look over her shoulder but Bob's head was turned as he backed away. She waited until he was out of sight, then drove her own car to the sheriff's station. The parking lot was empty and she remembered that the night dispatcher had taken time off with a sick baby. Any emergency calls would be rerouted to her cell phone. Linda was grateful for the privacy, the time alone. She powered up her computer and ran a search through the state law enforcement software and websites, then ran a series of public searches. She made two phone calls that confirmed what she'd learned about Alice and the firm that employed her. Then she called Alice at home and confronted her with the information. Alice resisted at first but came clean.

Linda locked the office and drove home. Inside she found Mick cleaning his Beretta at the kitchen table. It was old Formica with tarnished metal trim. She sat at one end.

"You fire your weapon?" she said.

"No, just habit. It focuses my mind, eyes, and hand. Gives the back of my brain a chance to percolate."

"Oh, man, big bro," she said. "You're getting deep as a puddle."

"You wearing date clothes?" he said.

"Not talking about it," she said. "It was nice, that's all."

She went to her room to change into her standard sweatpants and sweatshirt, what people now referred to as "lounge wear," a term that tickled her. It made her think of the game of *Clue*, which was where she'd learned the word "lounge." As far as she knew, no one in their family had ever lounged a minute of their lives. Mick was reassembling his weapon upon her return.

"There is something I need to talk about," she said.

He set the gun aside and waited, eyes on hers, a passive expression on his face.

"I got discharged from rehab," she said.

"Great. The job is yours. You'll need a deputy."

"Hold your horses, it doesn't go into effect immediately. Thing is, I was pushed out early. The physical therapist acted mighty squirrely and I asked Dr. Bob about it. You won't believe what he found out."

"I believe anything these days."

"It wasn't the therapist's idea. She told Bob that her boss made her do it. Guess who the boss answers to?"

"The governor?"

"Worse," she said. "Murvil Knox."

Mick nodded, intrigued. He'd never met Knox, a former coal tycoon who was slippery as chopped melon. No matter what the corrupt politicians said, big coal was on the way out. Knox had lost half his fortune to lawsuits over mountaintop removal. Next, he'd financed an undertaking to dispose of hazardous waste that took an illegal and violent turn. Knox had barely evaded indictment, which Mick figured cost millions.

"Murvil Knox," he said. "Did he pressure her to release you?"

"Not him personally. I called Alice at home. Someone who works for Knox was waiting for her in the hospital parking lot. She works out of a clinic in Lexington where some medicine had gone missing. Narcotics. Everyone's under suspicion. Knox's guy, he told Alice he knew it wasn't her who stole the drugs. But it would be easy to pin it on her. Unless she discharged me early."

"She told you all that?"

"Most of it. I think she was a little drunk and felt guilty."

"How'd she know that guy was working for Knox?"

"The stupid son of a bitch was driving a car with a parking sticker for Knox's new company in Frankfort. Sticker said 'Blue Moon Holdings.' She told Bob. I stopped by the station and looked into it. Owned by a company owned by Knox."

"Do you think she stole the drugs?"

"No idea. But it doesn't matter. The accusation would mess up her career."

Mick nodded, thinking it all through. He worked backward in his head, trying to figure out how ending Linda's rehabilitation would help Knox.

"He wants you back on the job," Mick said.

"Why?"

"You have a professional relationship with him. He gave you money for your reelection campaign."

"He thinks I owe him? Wants to collect?"

"Might be another reason, not about you so much."

"What do you mean?"

"Maybe he wants me out of the way."

"Why?"

"Knox knows I put the Feds on him over that toxic waste scheme. Could be he's up to something else. Doesn't want me after him again."

"Like what?" she said.

"No idea. But he likes big money stuff. Any of that around?"

"The biggest thing lately has been the hydroponic greenhouse. High tech, state of the art, all that bullshit. They call it a data-driven farm. Robots. No pesticides. They don't even use dirt, just man-made fertilizer. Lot of folks think they're getting ready for when the state legalizes weed."

"You believe that?" Mick said.

"Doesn't matter. It's an old pattern. New people come in, throw some money around, and take the profits out of state. Poor folks here do the work and rich folks get richer somewhere else."

"You think Knox is in on that?"

"I don't know. Blue Moon is an investment group. Could be anything. Pharmaceuticals. Private security. Real estate. Cyber whatever. Legal weed farm. The whole thing pisses me off. I been working my ass off to get back to work and now that I can, I don't trust the reason why. So dumb."

"No," Mick said. "You're second-guessing. Questioning. It's what makes you a good cop."

"I'm not a cop, I'm a damn sheriff."

"Like what Babe Ruth said when someone criticized him for smoking a cigar in public. 'I'm not an athlete, I'm a ballplayer.'"

"Didn't know you were a baseball fan."

"I'm not. A buddy told me that once. He read biographies of experts in their fields. He thought it might help. You know, crossover advice."

"Biographies of experts?" Linda said. "Did reading them help your buddy any?"

"I don't know. He died when our Jeep blew up."

"Maybe he should have read about an expert Jeep driver."

Mick stared at the pistol partially disassembled on the table.

"I was driving," he said.

"I'm sorry, Mick. It was a dumb joke. I'm getting tired."

"Big meal. Big date. You staying here?"

"No. Where's Ray-Ray at anyhow?"

"He goes out to practice his night vision."

"Can you practice that?"

"I guess so. You can fall out of the habit, I know that for sure. But it doesn't take long for me to get it back."

"Because you grew up in the damn woods. How's the cabin coming along?"

"Slow. When I show up they work pretty hard. You wanting to move back in here?"

"Soon, yeah," she said. "Shifty's was okay when Ray-Ray and J. C. were getting along. Now that damn Albin's out there running his mouth. Shifty turns up the TV to drown him out. I tried a podcast that was supposed to make me calm. Didn't work. I got irritated by how boring it was."

"My cabin's livable now, but I'd rather wait till they're done with Sheetrock. Give me a week and I'll be out of your hair."

"I'm not trying to get rid of you."

"I know it. But still. It's your place and your job. I'm supposed to be in Corsica."

"Right. Enjoying your 'retirement.' What the fuck does that even mean?"

"Guess I'll find out," Mick said. "Maybe I'll listen to podcasts."

They laughed together as if they were momentarily children.

Chapter Thirteen

The wood handle of the mattock cracked one afternoon and Johnny Boy figured he could fix it with wire, light nails, or heavy tape—none of which he could find. He went up the road to Sebastien's, stood in his waiting spot, and walked back. Sebastien didn't appear and Johnny Boy returned twice more with no luck. The third time he walked around the stone house to an area of scuffed earth with car tracks. The Renault was gone. He considered peeking into the dark windows but decided against it in case Sebastien came home and found him snooping.

Johnny Boy walked back down the road, smelling mint and juniper. He watched for his favorite local bird, a *guêpier d'Europe*, dazzling in its flight due to the brilliant colors—a bright blue breast, orange body, and yellow neck. Strips of black lay over its eyes like a bandit's mask. None were in sight today and Johnny Boy finished his work using the shovel. He was inside reading when Sebastien arrived.

"*Bonjour*," Johnny Boy said. "*Ça va?*"

"Don't walk behind my house again. It's not safe."

"What do you mean, not safe?"

"It's not safe for you," Sebastien said.

"All right. Sorry, buddy."

"There's activity. You need to stay away from my place. Keep yourself to yourself."

"The mattock broke."

"Show me."

Johnny Boy displayed the crack that ran along the handle. Sebastien tested it against the hard soil, feeling the wood bend at the weak point. He stared at Johnny Boy with his unwavering eyes, pale blue and hard as agate. In contrast his voice was gentler than usual.

"No matter what," he said, "you don't know me. You never saw me. You never heard of me. Follow?"

"Yeah, all right. I follow, okay? What about the village?"

"Unsafe."

"What's going on?"

"Movement."

Sebastien walked abruptly away, ignoring the road, and walking swiftly overland as if veering on an invisible path through the spikey scrub and rock. A string of cloud passed across the sun. In the diffused and translucent light, Sebastien vanished as if he'd stepped into a hole. It occurred to Johnny Boy that Sebastien was using the cloud shadow as concealment. He either anticipated the shifting light or reacted immediately from instinct. He'd disappeared like a magician's trick.

Sebastien's warning was clear and Johnny Boy would obey, but maybe the man was suffering from a flare of paranoia. He wondered what Sebastien meant by "there's movement." A political movement, a rebellion. Or tectonic shifts that risked a landslide. Most likely, Sebastien was a criminal. According to Titus, the island of Corsica had a long and dramatic history of sheltering pirates, thieves, and fugitives from the law. He recalled what Mick had told him—Sebastien was a former British soldier turned French Legionnaire. Maybe he had enemies from war. Regardless, Johnny Boy would avoid his house as well as the café, which meant no French lessons. He read Dumas, ate a light supper, and went to sleep.

In the morning, an intact mattock leaned against the handle of the outside well. Johnny Boy worked most of the day. He confined his perambulation to the immediate area surrounding the house. Three hogs wandered by. A light rain briefly cooled the air, offering a respite from effort and sweat, afterward releasing a fresh scent he couldn't place. He tracked the sharp tang to a low bush that spread wiry boughs across the soil as if snugging itself close to the earth.

As a teenager Johnny Boy had worked briefly at a fast-food franchise, toiling in the cramped kitchen where everything risked a cut or a burn. Corsica was oddly similar—a world of spiked plants, sharp stones protruding from the hot dirt, and the necessity of slow movement to prevent stumbling. He worked hard to sleep better, but time barely moved. He thought of an old song by the Clash with its lyrics about work: "The minutes drag and the hours jerk." Johnny Boy couldn't even grasp a minute going by.

He tipped the wheelbarrow against an exterior wall at the rear of the house and used the rough stone to climb onto the roof, testing its resilience as he moved. The thin shakes of stone were solid. At the peak he lay on the warm rock, peered over the ridge, and surveilled a foreign land of green and red with an unfamiliar contour. It was not his world. He was in it but not of it. He was like a wandering ghost seeking solid ground. The fundamentals were the same—dirt, tree, sky, rock, cloud—but he felt as if he were floating. Now, prone on the rough stone roof, the sensation was more natural, his body pressed at an angle by gravity.

He dozed, awakened by the shrill cry of a falcon. Dizzy from the sun, he climbed down slowly, misjudged the position of the wheelbarrow, and fell the last few feet. Unhurt, he laughed for the first time in weeks. Who else had ever gone to sleep on a roof? He felt trapped in some kind of middle ground between what had been and what was now. It was a liminal life, straddling two boundaries, but being part of neither. The uncertainty of his future assailed him like a horsewhip. All he knew how to do was work, eat, sleep, and try not to think.

For the rest of the day, he used the new mattock to break the hard crust of topsoil, then shoveled it into the wheelbarrow. West of the house was his pile of dirt, rock, and severed roots. Avoiding the village and café gave him a few more hours to himself in the afternoon, which he devoted to spreading the dump pile into a more uniform surface. A kind of make-work, he thought, but all of it was.

He napped briefly, which kept him awake in the evening. The night air was clear and he sat outside gazing at the black velvet sky. The Milky Way was a bright swath like trim on a fancy coat. Two stars lacked the glimmer of a twinkle and he assumed they were planets, one low to the horizon. He resolved to ask Sebastien for a guidebook to the constellations until he remembered the agreement to steer clear of his host. Whatever he was up to, it was none of Johnny Boy's business. A reliable deputy in his former life, he was good at following orders. Finally something felt familiar.

Chapter Fourteen

Mick sat in his office, ostensibly doing paperwork, but actually trying to figure out a diplomatic way to inform Chief Logan of Zack's innocence without giving up Patricia Holloway as his alibi. It was a mess. Everything was. Living in his sister's house, helping his ex-wife's reckless husband, and pouring his army retirement money into his grandfather's cabin. After haranguing himself a few minutes, he decided to concentrate on something more uplifting but couldn't come up with much. It was a pretty day out. So far, he'd made no overt mistakes.

The official phone on Sandra's desk had rung several times and Mick heard her gentle placations, which meant none of the calls were an emergency. The petty dramas of citizens: a lost dog, a loose cow, a tree branch in the road, a suspicious vehicle. The phone rang again and he listened to Sandra's voice shift to a serious tone. She cradled the old phone and appeared in his doorway, posture forthright, shoulders squared, face taut. He knew the information was no good.

"That was Trevor Johnston," she said. "A rough-out carpenter. Says he found a dead man. His boss. A contractor named Oscar Cook."

"Where?"

"Dry Creek Road. About a mile past the church graveyard is all he said. On the left."

Mick nodded and stood.

"One thing," she said. "Ray-Ray's out that direction. He can get there faster."

"All right. Tell Raymond I'll meet him there. I got to see Chet first. Looks like Zack's off the hook."

The conversation with Chief Logan went the way Mick expected—the secret alibi from an unnamed party went over like a snake in a chicken house. Chet was irritated because the investigation would have to start fresh. Despite his misgivings, Chet trusted Mick, who explained his theory that someone shot Skeeter in the bar, possibly twice. Skeeter fled out the front and received the fatal bullet in the parking lot. He'd died in the city limits but the initial assault took place inside the bar, which meant county jurisdiction.

Slightly mollified by the possibility that it was the sheriff's case, Chet sent two people to Ajax to take samples of the blood Mick had found. He'd fast-track the analysis to learn if it belonged to Skeeter.

"What about Zack Jones?" Mick said. "You kicking him loose?"

"Ain't got much choice. No physical evidence or murder weapon. You're sure about his whereabouts?"

"Solid."

Chet frowned and shook his head.

"I heard there's a shooting," he said. "Up Dry Creek."

"Raymond's on it. I'm heading over there now."

"How's Ray-Ray working out?"

"So far, so good. He closed his first case. Trespasser
in a barn."

"Kids?"

"A deer."

Chet grinned, a brief flare that returned fleeting joy
to his face.

"I'll let you know about the blood," Chet said.

Mick nodded and left. As he drove out of town, he
considered calling Peggy to tell her she'd need to retrieve
Zack from jail. The impulse was generous, he supposed, but
probably an excuse to demonstrate that he could still fix her
problems. No, he decided, better to avoid further contact.
She'd tossed him aside. It had been the worst pain in his life,
reignited by seeing her in the office. Maybe Mick had been
a sap all along, trapped by his own generosity that was now
aimed at the very person who'd hurt him most. He'd never
learned to be nice to himself, only others. He wondered if
that's why he spent so much time alone.

Dry Creek Road was in the small community known
as Dry Creek, which still had a post office, elementary
school, and a few businesses. He passed a car detailing place

and a handmade sign that offered stump grinding. The hills seemed to tighten around the road as he progressed deeper into the land. Weeds and saplings grew from cracks in the blacktop. He slowed for a box turtle crossing the road. People ate turtle but Mick's grandfather had refused, saying you can't trust any creature that never cleaned its own house. And that meant people, too.

A few miles later Mick found the early stage of a construction site. A concrete slab lay in place. The wooden forms had been removed and were lying in a jumble like a giant game of pick-up-sticks. Surrounding the site were tiny plastic flags of different colors to indicate routes for electric, sewer, and water lines. Mick wondered how many houses were planned for the site. Raymond's county SUV was parked off to the side, away from any tire tracks. Beyond it was a new extended cab pickup with dual rear wheels and an older Ford truck. The door was open and a man sat sideways with his boots on the dirt. His face was pale. Both arms were pressed to his stomach, his hands enfolding his rib cage in an awkward self-hug.

Mick parked just off the blacktop and walked past the county vehicle, careful to avoid the overlapping footprints in the dirt. A fresh set made a wide arc that ended at Raymond standing with the patience of an oak enduring hard weather. At his feet was the body of a man lying face down in dried blood.

"Dead as a doornail," Raymond said.

"Guy in the other truck?"

"He vomited up half his guts and called it in."

Raymond lifted a plastic evidence bag.

"Here's the pocket litter," Raymond said. "Wallet, gas receipt, roll of Lifesavers, unused tissue, toothpicks, and nicotine gum. All laying on the ground beside him. Somebody searched him."

"No keys?" Mick said.

"In the ignition. A loaded Glock in the glove box. Registration matches the driver's license. Oscar Cook. He ain't cooking no more."

Mick nodded, understanding that the grim humor was a means to accommodate the emotional distance necessary at a murder scene.

"One other thing," Raymond said. "His wallet has six hundred forty-seven dollars in it. Not robbery."

"Maybe a car drove by or the killer was in a hurry. Or he found what he was looking for. You touch him?"

"No. I don't know the protocol."

"I don't either. But out here we're the law."

Mick used his cell phone to photograph the corpse at different angles, including close-ups of the hand and back of his head. He stepped back to align the road and truck for scale and distance. Raymond pointed to a set of footprints that went toward the woods.

"I'm going to follow those," Raymond said. "Might lead to a vehicle's escape route."

Mick nodded. He squatted to photograph the dead man's boot tread, a way to rule out his tracks. It was probably a waste of time because there were dozens of footprints, old and new, from various work crews. Using a series of rocks, he marked the right side of the corpse, then grasped the hips and rolled it over. Oscar Cook was in his forties with a heavy mustache, an attempt to make his delicate features appear tougher. He'd been shot three times in the torso and once in the neck. Mick stepped back and took more photos. From the tree line he heard Raymond whistle twice.

"Mick," he called. "Got another one."

Mick walked parallel to Raymond's tracks beside another set of footprints. The stride began to extend, the heel coming down harder, leaving a deeper half-moon crevice in the dirt. Someone had started to run. The earth dipped to a gully. Mick followed a loose trail of bent saplings and broken weeds to a tree blown down by a storm, its large root ball protruding six feet from the earth like a tombstone. Behind it was a second body, a young man with long brown hair. He'd been crouching in the shallow hole left by the root ball. Shot twice in the back, he'd fallen forward against the rounded wall of dirt, then slid sideways as if placing himself in a makeshift grave.

Raymond stepped into the woods, producing just enough sound that Mick knew he was moving back and forth in arcs beneath the canopy of limbs. The noise faded as he got farther away. Mick eased a wallet from the man's pocket. Ronald Morris was twenty-two years old. He had eight dollars, a credit card, and a driver's license. The slenderness of the wallet made his death sadder. Mick studied the name, Ronald Homer Morris. Ronnie. The address matched the official call he'd made a couple of days before—the house with the yurt in the backyard.

The slight rustle of sweetgum leaves indicated Raymond's return. He stepped from the woods as if the trees themselves had released him.

"Nobody there," Raymond said. "But plenty of sign. Somebody circled around behind that boy and killed him."

"Any physical evidence?"

"Nothing. Not a footprint or a shell casing. Bent over grass and broke sticks is about it. Whoever it was knew how to move in the woods."

"That takes in half the county," Mick said.

Raymond climbed the slope and stood beside Mick. They stared at the body, its face visible in a narrow spray of sunlight.

"Barely started shaving," Raymond said. "What do you make of it?"

"Two options. Both were the target. Or one was and the other a witness. Searching the first man makes him more likely the target. This boy saw the shooting and ran. Hid behind that tree root."

"Should've gone down that hill and followed the creek."

"Maybe he didn't know the land," Mick said. "Or got slowed down somehow."

Raymond squatted beside the corpse and inspected the hands. Both palms had abrasions running lengthwise from the fingertips to the wrist. The knees of his pants were streaked with dried mud and grass stains.

"He fell," Raymond said. "Maybe twice."

"You get anything out of the other guy?"

"Nothing. All he's done is cry."

"Dig around in that tree root and see if there's a round that went through this kid."

Mick climbed the hill to the construction site. Above the rich green tree line were a series of cumulus clouds shaped like cauliflowers, detached from each other as if deliberately occupying their own space. A crow landed in a tree, then another. Mick thought they'd taken their own sweet time. The buzzards would arrive soon. He walked to the Ford truck, which was dented on all sides. A sheet of plywood lay in the bed, cut to fit around the wheel wells. Old Bondo had flaked off the rear fender, exposing the undercarriage. The driver was slumped over the steering wheel. At Mick's approach the man startled suddenly, spinning his body, and banged his head on the rearview mirror.

"You're all right," Mick said. "I'm the sheriff. Need to ask you a few things. Is that okay?"

"I done talked to that other boy."

"Yeah, he's deputy. You need to talk to me, too. Sorry, buddy, but that's the way these things go."

"Right now?" the man said. "I ain't feeling all that good."

"Best when it's fresh in your mind," Mick said. "You need any water?"

"I got some, thank ye."

"What's your name?"

"Leeroy Jenkins. You know, like the *World of Warcraft* guy."

Mick nodded, not understanding the reference, knowing it didn't matter. A witness to murder tended to ramble.

"All right, Leeroy. Tell me what happened up here."

"I don't know."

"I mean, when did you get here? Why did you come? Who all was already here?"

"I was meeting Oscar. He's the contractor on this. I'm a carpenter, second man on his crew. My daddy trained me up. He's passed now, but I use all his tools. Best hammer in the county."

"That's good," Mick said. "Nothing better than solid tools. Why were you meeting Oscar?"

"To see if the concrete was cured enough to start on the walls."

"Was it?"

"I don't know. I never checked. Got out of the truck and seen him laying there. At first I thought he'd slipped and fell. Then I saw the blood."

"Did you touch him?"

"Heck, no. I ran back to my truck and got sick. Then called y'all."

"You did the right thing," Mick said. "Was there anybody else up here?"

"Naw. Just me and him."

"What about another car or truck. Anything like that?"

"Uh-uh."

"You hear anything, Leeroy?"

"Like what?"

"Car engine. Gunshots."

"No, nothing. He's dead, ain't he?"

Mick nodded. Leeroy's face blanched white as a new T-shirt. He tried to get out of the truck and stumbled. Mick caught his arm and held him while he retched. Nothing came up. His knees wobbled. Mick eased him to the ground and leaned his back against the front tire, shaded by the hood of the truck.

"Put your head between your legs," Mick said. "Sip water but don't gulp it. I'll be back in a minute."

Mick radioed Sandra and filled her in. He asked her to hurry the EMTs, notify the county coroner, and request assistance from Chief Logan. In the silence of death, the birds slowly returned to their song. The leaves of oak and hickory were pale green against the darker hues of maple and pine. The day was lovely.

Chapter Fifteen

Three hours later Mick sat in the foyer of the funeral home, waiting to talk with the county coroner about the bodies from the construction site. He wished he were in Corsica and wondered how Johnny Boy was getting along in his new life there. Probably rough as a cob. Mick grinned at the thought of Johnny Boy's incessant talk encountering Sebastien's powerful bulwark of silence.

Mick had met Sebastien in Afghanistan during a joint operation with British forces. Mick was temporarily detached to US Special Forces in a classified mission that also drew on the British Special Air Service. Mick was not accepted by the Delta troops and Sebastien was distant from everything, including his comrades in the SAS. After three days of each other's company traveling through rough terrain and avoiding the enemy, they begrudgingly acknowledged the other's abilities. They got along mainly because neither talked much.

During a brutal dust storm, their team hunkered down for twelve hours, then came under heavy fire from the Taliban, who were hiding behind dunes that hadn't existed before the storm. Two coalition soldiers were killed immediately. The survivors mounted a successful counterattack by charging the enemy. Mick was pinned down by gunfire and Sebastien came back. He picked off two enemies and applied field bandages to Mick's leg. They waited until darkness and began moving slowly when Taliban forces ambushed them. Sebastien was shot twice. Mick lay in the sand until the enemy were two yards away, then eliminated them as threats. He dressed Sebastien's wounds and they spent four days returning to safety, traveling at night, having essentially saved each other's lives. At the end of the secret mission, they maintained contact, although infrequently.

Later Mick received an invitation to the CIA but he'd already decided to join the Criminal Investigative Division of the US Army. Sebastien was recruited by MI6, the UK's foreign service, for a few particularly unsavory assignments. Disgruntled by politics, he resigned and joined the French Foreign Legion. As part of Operation Barkhane in the Sahel region, he sustained shrapnel wounds in combat. Having shed blood for France, he was offered French citizenship. Sebastien renounced his British citizenship and relocated to France. Mick had subsequently visited him in Corsica, the second most beguiling place he'd been other than Kentucky. If anyone could bring Johnny Boy back to himself, Sebastien could.

Marquis came down the hall, his crepe-soled shoes silent on the carpeted floor. Mick followed him to the morgue, which held its usual smell of industrial cleaner and embalming fluid. Two bodies lay on gurneys beneath draped cloths. Marquis slipped a heavy smock over his clothes and put on latex gloves. He moved slowly as if weary. Under his heavy eyes were dark crescents, the signs of little sleep.

"How long since you rested?" Mick said.

"I can't remember."

He consulted notes on a clipboard. His voice and manner had an exaggerated formal tone that Mick understood was a means to get through difficulties when exhausted. It was the same as Ray-Ray's rough humor. Marquis focused on his clipboard as he spoke.

"Both victims died four to eight hours ago. Mr. Cook was shot three times at close range. Mr. Collins from farther back. A thirty-eight bullet struck two ribs and lodged against his spine. I removed it. No defensive wounds on either man. Dirt under Mr. Collins's fingernails and on the right side of his face. Questions?"

"Raymond found a thirty-eight bullet in a tree root where Collins was. Think the one you found is from the same weapon?"

"No way to know till forensics comes back from Lexington. Chet put a rush on it, but they're backed up."

"Anything else? Something not right? Anomalies? Any speculation is off the record."

"The wounds in Mr. Cook are vertically perpendicular. He either fell as he was shot or the killer was raising the gun. Or lowering it as he fired. Mr. Collins's wounds are tight together. He barely moved."

"What's your gut say?"

"My gut says I'm wore down to a nub and hungry."

"Thanks, Marquis," Mick said. "Let me know when you hear from forensics."

Marquis gave a slight nod and Mick left. In the truck, he radioed Sandra that he was going to the Morris house.

"All right," she said. "Ray-Ray's still taking a formal statement from Leeroy Jenkins."

"Good. When he's done, tell him to find out what he can about Oscar Cook. Enemies. Disputes. The usual."

"Copy that."

Mick ended the call and headed out of town. Marquis had confirmed what Mick had suspected—both men were killed by the same caliber bullet. Skeeter died from a thirty-eight, too. It could be significant but a .38 pistol was common in the hills.

The old Pontiac was still in the yard at the Morris house. Mick parked beside it, surprised to see Loretta and Mrs. Morris sitting on the porch with the dog. He wished he had someone to accompany him. Delivering such awful news was better with two people—one to talk and one to offer sympathy. He walked across the grass, reminding himself to move slowly. The dog stood and barked, tail upright and wagging furiously.

"Conway," Mrs. Morris said. "You're okay."

The dog charged to meet Mick, then stopped short as if sensing the sadness of his visit. Mick stretched a hand to Conway as he walked. Mrs. Morris gestured to a third chair, added to the porch since he was last there.

"Come on up and sit a minute," Mrs. Morris said.

Mick stood at the bottom of the three board steps to the porch that fronted the house.

"I've got something to tell y'all," he said. "Can we go inside?"

"Out here's cooler," Mrs. Morris said. "We're good now. Loretta has been learning me up on the tarot. I even drank some kombucha!"

Mick stepped onto the bottom step.

"It's about Ronnie," he said. "We found a body."

The women stared at him without speaking. Conway stood between them, tail tucked.

"What?" Loretta said. "What do you mean? Ronnie's out getting a job on a construction site. Meeting the contractor."

"I'm really sorry," Mick said. "There was a shooting in the county. Two people. One was the contractor. The other man was Ronnie."

"Ronnie's dead?" Loretta said.

"Yes, ma'am. I'm very sorry."

Mrs. Morris hurled the glass of kombucha at Mick. He shifted his posture but it struck his shoulder, slinging the contents across his chest and face. He could hear it bouncing across the grass behind him. Mrs. Morris slumped in the chair. Conway began licking her hand.

"Are you sure?" Loretta said.

"The wallet was his. A city officer recognized him."

"How'd he know Ronnie? He's never been in trouble."

"The officer interviewed Ronnie at Ajax a few days ago."

Loretta stood and Mick braced himself for an attack. She walked past him to retrieve the empty glass from the yard. Her legs trembled. Mick took her arm and helped her back onto the porch, where she dropped into the chair as if her knees had given out. She gripped the glass tightly.

"Say my boy's dead?" Mrs. Morris said.

"Yes, ma'am. We'll need a formal identification. I'm really sorry. Is there someone I can call to come by? A relative or neighbor?"

"No. Get out. Get off my property. Don't come back here."

Mick nodded. He held the banister and walked backward down the steps to the grass. Loretta's face was pale. Mrs. Morris hugged her daughter-in-law. As Mick walked to his truck, he heard their weeping and knew it would continue for days, weeks, and months, then periodically for the rest of their lives.

He used a rag to wipe away the kombucha, the vinegary smell lingering on his clothes. He wondered if he could have handled it better. Probably, he thought. But he had no idea how. He drove half a mile, pulled over in a wide spot, and called the contractor who was renovating his grandfather's cabin. Wendell answered immediately.

"Hey, Mick," he said. "How do you like it?"

"Uh, what?"

"The cabin. I know we ain't full done, but good enough, right?"

"I don't know."

"Aw, buddy. Don't mess with me. I know you been out there."

"Not since last time, no."

"Somebody has."

"What do you mean?"

"There's stuff laying around inside. Figured it was you."

"Let's meet there. I need to talk to you about something. Probably owe you money anyhow."

Wendell agreed and hung up. Mick checked his wallet. He'd taken to carrying two loose checks in addition to forty dollars. Hill culture still operated in the traditional way of checks and cash, although Sandra had mentioned her niece used Venmo, then explained the process to Mick. It sounded like an electronic version of Hawala using your phone. He radioed Sandra as he drove.

"I'm following up with a contractor," he said. "Will you do me a favor and please ask Raymond to check on the Morrises?"

"You don't have to be polite," she said. "You're the sheriff. Just give the orders. It's a whole lot quicker."

"Yeah, okay. Sorry."

"And don't apologize."

Her transmission ended and Mick drove east, deeper into the hills. He'd worked with women many times, in the army as well as foreign militaries, but never at the high level of awkwardness as with Sandra. It wasn't their night of passion that had messed things up, but his failure to be in touch afterward. Instead he'd returned to base in Germany for a year, then spent another year at Fort Leonard Wood training young investigators. Now he was her superior officer and their history stood between them like a wall.

He went back through their conversation. All right, he thought, give orders and quit apologizing. He'd try but he was afraid she'd get upset about that, too. There it was—fear as his primary response to women and the threat of their anger. Seeking to avoid it had damaged his marriage irreparably. He pushed thoughts of Peggy aside. He wasn't pondering his marriage so much as his own ineptitude with women. Maybe the better response was to avoid women. He shook his head to himself. No, he knew many men who lived that way. Lonely and resentful, they withered from an isolation that cut years from their lives.

The road to his grandfather's cabin held a series of fresh and old tracks from various vehicles. At the top was Wendell's big four-door pickup truck with a gleaming steel lockbox bolted to part of the bed. The dimpled pattern in the metal reflected sunlight. Mick parked behind it.

Wendell stood at the cabin's front door with his cell phone on speaker, holding it away from him. Mick could hear a tinny voice rapidly speaking in an irritated tone.

Wendell was nodding, a fruitless phone habit Mick recognized as one of his own, then began gesturing. He said "Yes, sir" three times in a row, listened, then said it twice more and finally made a friendly farewell. He turned to Mick.

"Nothing ever goes right," Wendell said. "If it ain't the owners, it's the carpenters. If it ain't them, it's the suppliers. Evidently, my crew nailed a porch ceiling on upside down."

"A ceiling has two sides?"

"This one does. One side's smooth. The other side has grooved panels made to look like slats. The owner wants the slat side facing down and the lines to run the opposite way. Opposite of what, I don't know."

"Reckon you could take it down, flip it, and replace it."

"Could, yeah," Wendell said. "But it'll be cheaper to buy all-new material and put that up. Owner will get a sturdier ceiling at no extra cost. I'll wind up reminding him about that half a dozen times."

Mick stepped inside his cabin. The walls and ceiling were Sheetrocked and sanded, the seams covered by tape and compound. A two-sink unit was installed beside a small counter. Beside it was a cubicle for the refrigerator and stove with heavy-duty electrical sockets. Hardwood floors throughout, window frames in place. The contour of the space was the same as before the fire but everything else was new.

Two sleeping bags lay unrolled on the floor with pillows made from pants tucked inside T-shirts. Fast-food bags littered a corner along with cans of Spam, Vienna sausages, and half a box of crackers. Beside that were two jugs of water, one full, the other three-quarters empty. There were no beer cans or cigarette butts. No evidence of drug use. Whoever was squatting here wasn't kids. Maybe poachers hunting out of season or men taking a break from tense homes.

"This ain't you up here?" Wendell said.

"No. Maybe some of your work crew?"

"I checked. They all went home every day. Who do you think it is?"

"I don't know," Mick said. "What do I owe you?"

Wendell named a figure that would cover a payment up to the final ten percent. Mick wrote a check and carried it outside, Wendell following. A yellow finch streaked away from a perennial patch of black-eyed Susans.

"Oscar Cook," Mick said. "You know him?"

"Sure. He runs a bigger outfit than me. Maybe the biggest."

"What's the difference? More workers?"

"Kind of. He uses subcontractors with their own crews. I do jobs like yours. Smaller. Oscar, he gets on big commercial jobs. New construction. More money and a lot more headaches."

"Like that site up Dry Creek?"

"Yeah," Wendell said. "What they call a spec project. Build one house, lay out a road, run power and water. Wait on the first buyer."

"Anything else he into?"

"What I heard, he was a partner in a big development by the interstate. They're clearing out a trailer court and putting in new homes."

"Where's it at?"

"Beside where Long John Silver's used to be by the old flea market place. Know it?"

"I'll find it," Mick said. "Was it just Oscar on it?"

"Naw, there's a couple of money guys. Oscar's investment is labor. He tried to hire me and my crew. I wouldn't do it."

"Why not?"

"Couple of reasons," Wendell said. "First, I wouldn't get paid till way later. The big money guys would cover material and wages for my crew. But nothing for me or my time. Plus, I'd wind up losing out profit on other jobs, like yours. I got two more lined up. I'd rather go for the sure thing."

"What'd Oscar say to that?"

"Said I'd make a lot of money later."

"Are there problems with Oscar?"

"Naw, he's all right. What bugged me was him being cagey about the financing. Said there was a bar owner in on it but wouldn't say who. And a coal guy, you know, one of those big operators so crooked he screws his britches on."

"Did he mention his name?"

"Murvil Knox. What's all this to you, Mick? I hope you ain't hiring Oscar over me on something out here."

"Oscar's dead."

"Shit. Accident on the job?"

"He got shot. Know anybody might be mad at him?"

"Those big contractors always got problems. Usually money. But he was easygoing, got along with folks. Half the job is that. He was good at it."

Mick gave him the check. Wendell demonstrated his trust by not looking at the amount as he slipped it inside his shirt pocket.

"You hear anything on Oscar," Mick said, "let me know."

Wendell nodded and drove away. Mick walked around the cabin, seeing the standard construction debris—scrap wood, pop bottles, and crumpled fast-food bags. Glinting among high weeds was a misplaced tri-square. He returned to the front of the cabin and studied the ground but couldn't discern any vehicle tracks that were newer than the others. One set went a little farther than the rest and ended at a pile of brush, which was unusual. There should have been a corresponding pair of curved tracks when the car backed up and turned around, but Mick saw none. He circled the brush pile and found a car covered with small branches and leaves, a crude but relatively effective means of camouflage. It was a gray Impala with Michigan plates. Mick knew the car and who drove it.

He returned to his pickup and honked the horn.

"Vernon," he yelled. "Come on out. It's Mick. I'm alone."

Mick had ridden in the Impala several months ago while investigating a witness. Vernon worked for Charley Flowers, a crime boss in Detroit. Vernon's family had moved to Michigan decades ago, part of the Appalachian out-migration for employment, and he still had relatives in Eldridge County. If Vernon was squatting here with a hidden car, he had a big problem in Michigan. And Mick owed his boss a favor.

A blue jay flew from a sycamore to a sugar maple and landed on an upper bough that swayed from its weight. The jay gave a warning squawk and the other birds hushed. Within a minute Mick heard tramping among the trees, the clumsy sound of a human with no wood skills. He directed his vision at a natural gap in the trees. The noise increased and Vernon emerged from the gap, followed by another man, short and wide, his clothes loose to accommodate powerful muscles. His hair was shiny black in a kind of bowl cut as if the barber had used a deep flowerpot. He wore a black shirt and a web harness for a nine-millimeter Glock. Vernon stepped into the light.

"Hidy, Vernon," Mick said.

"Anybody else here?" Vernon said.

"Just me. I found the car. You and your buddy can come up here and tell me what's going on."

Vernon gestured to the other man.

"This here's Cro," Vernon said.

"Crow," Mick said. "On account of his black hair?"

"Not Crow," Vernon said. "Cro. Like Cro-Magnon."

Cro shrugged his heavy shoulders, a motion that disturbed the air.

"Uh-huh," Mick said. "Why are you here?"

Vernon glanced at Cro, who shrugged. It was a different movement than before and Mick wondered if there was a secret eloquence to his shoulders, a vestige from the past. Maybe the Cro-Magnon people had gone extinct due to a lack of verbal language.

"Charley sent us," Vernon said. "It's a mess up there. A war. Me and Cro were targets. Charley told us to drive straight here and hide out."

"Are you down here recruiting? I can't leave. I'm the sheriff now."

"You got upped from deputy?"

"Long story, Vernon. Anybody know you're here?"

"Not supposed to. But guys know I'm from Eldridge County. Don't worry, nobody will ever find this place."

"What ain't you telling me?" Mick said.

"Charley said to say that us being here was calling in his favor. Said you'd know what he meant."

"Yeah, I do," Mick said. "Y'all can stay here long as you need to. How come you didn't call me?"

"Charley said not to use the phones. Might get tracked."

"I'll make sure no more carpenters come up here. Kids might, teenagers. Don't fuck with them and they'll leave. You did the right thing hiding the car."

Despite Vernon's tough ways, he was still an overgrown kid who brightened under the unexpected compliment.

"You're pretty squared away in there," Mick said. "Neat and tidy, I mean. Was Cro in the military?"

"Yeah," Vernon said. "Then prison."

Cro delivered a different shrug that Mick couldn't interpret.

"There's plenty of well water," Mick said. "How you fixed for food?"

"Running a little low."

"I'll try to get some groceries. Might take a while. I'm in the middle of a few murders."

"Us, too."

Vernon chuckled and Cro's shoulders twitched. Mick nodded to each man, got in his truck, and drove to the blacktop.

Chapter Sixteen

By midday Johnny Boy had sweated through his work shirt and was letting it dry while he rested inside. The whine of an automobile engine drifted through the stone walls, then stopped. Johnny Boy dressed quickly in his spare shirt and stepped outside, expecting the old red Renault. A couple in their thirties were leaning against a blue car of a model Johnny Boy didn't recognize—stubbed at both ends as if perfectly pressed between a giant vise. They were studying a map unfolded on the car's hood. At the sound of the house door closing, they looked at him. The man appeared puzzled and the woman smiled broadly.

"*Bonjour,*" she said. "*Nous sommes perdus. Peux-tu s'il te plait nous aider?*"

Johnny Boy did his best to translate in his head but failed. He recognized a few words, but her accent was different from Titus, his teacher, or any of the villagers with whom he spoke.

"*Bonjour*," Johnny Boy said. "*Je m'appelle Jean. Je parle un peu le français.*"

"Oh, I am Sabrina," she said in English. "You are American?"

"Yep."

Her tone took on a fresh enthusiasm and cheer.

"We are Swiss," she said. "Corsica is the most beautiful place. We were here five years ago for our *voyage de noces.* Honeymoon. Now we are back! And we are a little bit lost. *C'est dommage.*"

Johnny Boy approached them, eager for company and the chance to talk English. Both appeared physically fit, wearing loose clothing and hiking shoes. The man was slightly older, his skin dark from exposure to the elements.

"This is Fabian," she said.

Fabian smiled without showing his teeth and gave a nod. His eyes had an intense aspect as if able to look through Johnny Boy and into the house behind him.

"Have you been to Switzerland?" Fabian said.

"No, never," Johnny Boy said. "I had a pocketknife from there. Good knife."

"Oh yes," Sabrina said. "All the world knows the Swiss army knife, our chocolate, and watches. We have the longest tunnel in the world. That is what we are known for."

The man and woman laughed lightly. Johnny Boy nodded, not quite understanding the joke.

"We are working on a book," she said with more exuberance. "A tourist guide. For Swiss and Germans. We want to include the perspectives and experiences of expats."

"Expats?" Johnny Boy said.

"Expatriates. People who relocate here from another country. Have you lived here long?"

"Not really," Johnny Boy said.

"Is it difficult to live in Corsica?"

"Lonely, mainly."

"And what's up the road?" Sabrina said.

"It dead-ends at a house."

"Is it for rent?"

"I don't know."

"Who lives there?"

"I haven't seen anybody."

"Perhaps it is a vacation home," Fabian said to her. "We could include it in the guide?"

"Folks in the village," Johnny Boy said, "they'll know more than me."

The man began folding the map, his movements crisp and sharp as if he'd handled hundreds of maps. He got behind the wheel of the little car. Sabrina continued to smile pleasantly, glancing around at the land.

"It is very peaceful," she said. "What do you do with your time?"

"I read and do a little work. Sometimes I go to the village and practice French. That helps. But it's real nice to talk English with y'all."

"And nice for us," she said. "Thank you. *Merci*."

"You're welcome. *De rien*."

She maneuvered herself around the car with the efficient grace of an athlete and they drove up the hill toward Sebastien's house. Proud of himself for using rudimentary French with strangers, Johnny Boy changed into his work clothes. The new mattock had a slimmer handle that required a slight adjustment of grip that rubbed fresh blisters below his calluses. He wrapped strips of rag around his palms and was loosening a large rock when the Swiss couple drove slowly by. Sabrina was waving and smiling while Fabian concentrated on the road. Johnny Boy lifted his arm in farewell until the car receded down the hill and the red dust of its passage had settled fully to the earth.

He sipped water while thinking about getting married in one country and traveling to another for a honeymoon. What was the point? Romantic and significant, he supposed. Now they'd returned to commemorate an anniversary. Perhaps he'd appear in their guide—the friendly American in sweat-stained clothes. He was glad he'd not given his full name, because he'd lied and already felt bad about it.

Lying was not natural to Johnny Boy. A reliance on honesty and fairness through direct communication had always assisted him in law enforcement. Nevertheless, Johnny Boy had lied on Sebastien's behalf simply because he'd requested it and he wondered if the Swiss writers could tell. Probably not. Different culture, language, and way of being. Falsehoods would offer equally different clues of face and tone. It didn't matter. Nothing mattered but getting through each day, then admiring the few square feet of dirt that was smoother than before. He was living in increments, a small life marked by even smaller moments. The Swiss writers were a dazzling break from the monotony.

He worked, cleaned his tools, and ate a supper of ham, cucumber, and tomato. After watching the night sky for half an hour, he went in the house, where a lantern spread a dim light across the thin pages of a novel he'd borrowed from Sebastien. *The Count of Monte Cristo* was a complicated adventure story of a man imprisoned for fourteen years on a Mediterranean island north of Corsica. He escaped, became rich, and inflicted terrible vengeance on the men who had sent him to prison. Johnny Boy enjoyed the book, though he read slowly, often rereading the formal language, awkward to his mental ear. The themes of loyalty, revenge, despair, and occasional mercy reminded him of the hills of Kentucky. He closed the book, extinguished the lantern, and went to sleep hoping that his own exile would not last fourteen years.

A sound awoke him abruptly—an explosion from somewhere in the night, muffled but close. Still half asleep he thought he was back home hearing men hunting raccoons at night. He stepped outside. The moon was low and to the east. Nothing was visible but he could smell cordite drifting on the black air. A minute passed and he heard the crunch of rock, a scraping against the earth. He stepped into

the shadow of the house and cut the light, expecting to see
a wild boar someone had shot at.

Stumbling along the road were the Swiss writers dressed
in black. The woman supported the man, who was barely
able to walk. His left arm dangled loosely and his left leg
dragged along the ground like a heavy broom. He grunted
with each step but the woman was moving him fast. She
hunched her shoulder to regain control of the hurt man and
take more of his weight.

Johnny Boy stepped into the light, prepared to offer
help. He heard their gasping breath.

"Hey," he said. "Do you—"

"*Nein, nichts,*" the woman said. "*Bleib weg.*"

The harsh language was unintelligible but Johnny Boy
understood the hostile timbre of her voice. He watched
their progress down the road until they became silhouettes
and the rattle of rocks kicked by their passage dwindled to
silence. He wondered where they'd parked their car and
why they were walking. He was unsure of what to do, a
powerlessness he didn't like. It sparked all his despair and
sorrow at what his life had become.

He went inside the house, propped the door wide, and
moved his lone chair to the opening. Unable to sleep, he
kept watch until dawn. In the gorgeous, streaming light he
inspected the road and found arcs of drying blood made by
the man's wounded leg sweeping over the earth with each
step. There were no spurts to indicate a severed artery. He'd
probably live but something had torn him up pretty bad.

The pair had come from the direction of Sebastien's house. They were burglars, he decided, not writers, casing the area for empty homes. Sebastien had ordered him to stay away and he resolved to rest. In the stronger light of full day, he'd seek an overland route to Sebastien's house for a visual angle from a distance. He lay in his clothes and slept a few hours.

After coffee and bread, he went back outside to the road. The dried blood was gone. Not a single small stone showed a speck of red. He searched in the direction of the village and found nothing, as if the blood trail had never existed. No footprints in the dust. Maybe he'd dreamed it all, a nightmare of trauma released from the crevices of his brain in sleep. Had the Swiss couple truly visited him yesterday afternoon? Was he losing his mind in the heat and solitude? Had they murdered him and this was a form of afterlife? It felt hellish enough—boring, repetitive, hot. He recalled something he'd read in a book about Winston Churchill. "When you're going through hell, keep going." Johnny Boy had forgotten the context but it didn't matter because he had nowhere else to go. This was where he'd gone to.

Despite Sebastien's clear orders, he climbed the road toward his house in a partial crouch, scanning the earth. Still nothing, no sign of human passage, not even a partial tread from the strange little blue car. He went to his waiting spot and stood in the overhead sun, sweat gathering in his eyebrows until it spilled onto his lids and into his eyes. He wondered if it was possible to trim the brows in such a way as to channel lines of perspiration to the side of his face. Maybe he could apply wax to form a furrow like a gutter. Someone must have tried it. He heard nothing until Sebastien spoke behind him.

"Jean," he said softly.

Startled, Johnny Boy spun to Sebastien, who stood six feet away as if he'd dropped silently from the sky or grown suddenly from the dry soil. Johnny Boy had never known anyone capable of such stillness. Mick was quiet in the woods but not like Sebastien on the rocky ground.

"What happened last night?" Johnny Boy said. "I saw them go by."

"A probe."

"There was blood in the road this morning."

"They were never here."

"They said they were writing a guidebook."

Sebastien didn't respond.

"Wanted to know if anyone else lived up here," Johnny Boy said. "I said no."

"Good man."

"Will they be back?"

"Not them," Sebastien said.

"Somebody else?"

After half a minute, Sebastien nodded once, the first movement during their conversation.

"What do you want me to do?" Johnny Boy said.

"Nothing. Do everything you normally do. Go to the village as usual."

"What do they want?"

Sebastien's expression remained the same, his steady gaze unblinking. The Swiss man, Fabian, had the same trait, as if looking through flesh, trees, and walls—missing nothing. The two men were similar but how had they learned such an odd skill? It occurred to Johnny Boy that he could learn it himself.

"I'll tell you when it's safe," Sebastien said. "Off you go now."

Thus dispatched, Johnny Boy walked along the road, trying without success to make no sound. He worked the rest of the day. He slept hard that night and went to the village the next afternoon. Titus greeted him warmly as if there'd been no break in their visits. He served a meal and afterward Madame Moncoso arrived for lessons. Time seemed to have shifted again, to have no meaning. Johnny Boy wasn't sure how many days he'd skipped his solitary journeys to the village and his feeble conversations in French. None of it felt real but he knew it was. Sebastien had confirmed it. A probe, he said. Johnny Boy didn't know what that meant aside from an electrical test or maybe medical.

Chapter Seventeen

As Mick drove to town from his cabin, he made a call to Wendell, postponing all further work, and to Raymond, who didn't answer. He called Sandra, remembering her advice of not apologizing or explaining.

"Raymond's not answering," he said.

"He's on a call way up Lower Lick Holler. No reception."

"Right. I'm on my way to . . ."

Mick realized he didn't know where he was headed and ended the call. He'd never taken case notes in the field, a precaution for combat zones that was less applicable in the hills, especially with three murders. He mentally reviewed what little he knew—dead bar owner with documents missing from his safe, dead contractor with money left behind, dead kid looking for day work. For most investigators the rule of thumb was to focus on any coincidence, but Ronnie's death seemed like the bad luck of being in the wrong place at the wrong time. Collateral damage.

Mick's onboard computer dinged twice, reminding him of an old-time doorbell. Sandra's voice was terse.

"Ray-Ray's got a wounded man," she said. "Ambulance is on the way. Wait. Hang on."

Mick rolled the window down while he waited. Four finches lifted from the boughs of a maple and fled like yellow tracer rounds. He watched them vanish into the green gauze of leaves. Sandra's tinny voice returned.

"Ray-Ray's got the shooter, too. A woman."

"Name?"

"She wouldn't give it. Said she'll only talk to you."

Maybe it was the sister of a buddy he hadn't seen for twenty-five years. In Eldridge County so few people completed high school that it never really ended, the relationships of loyalty and resentment that were forged as teens continued to the grave. He'd have to pretend to remember the woman.

"Okay," Mick said. "What's the location?"

"No address," she said. "Go up Lick Creek, then left at the fork. That's Lower Lick Road. Used to be an old walking bridge there. You know it?"

"Aren't they all walkable?"

"I mean one of those old-timey kinds. Just boards and ropes for one person to cross on."

"Right," Mick said. "I know it. Goes to the old Branham place. Three sisters lived there. Supposed to be haunted."

"What's not in these hills?"

"I've thought the same thing. When I was a kid I wondered if my future ghost could haunt me."

"Maybe it is now," Sandra said. "Maybe you're a ghost. I mean, we're talking and can't see each other."

"Uh, right. Didn't mean to get philosophical."

"Don't apologize."

"Where's the turnoff for the bridge?"

"It's just past the place where your cell signal stops. Go left. If you see an old barn fallen in, you went too far. Got it?"

"Yeah."

He put the truck in gear and headed across the county, a long and meandering drive through the labyrinth of slanted hillsides and slender dead-end hollers. Half an hour later, the blacktop narrowed to a single lane with cracks forming a mosaic in the brittle tar. He saw the remnants of a barn with a collapsed roof, the framing covered by vines. Five poplars grew from the center of the dirt foundation, the soil rich from hay and horse manure. According to Sandra's directions, he'd missed the turnoff. He drove back until he saw a vague opening in the heavy brush with fresh tire marks. Drooping fronds of willow concealed the entry, but also indicated wet ground. Concerned that the old pickup might get stuck if the road dipped into a creek, he parked and walked.

The road ended at a field of ryegrass and fescue high as Mick's waist, each blade edged with seed. A haze of pollen drifted east like water. A car and a Dodge Ram truck were visible near the county vehicle, in which a figure sat hunched in the back seat. Raymond stood a few feet away, aiming his cell phone at the sky and turning in a circle to seek reception.

"Just trying to get hold of you," Raymond said.

"What've you got?"

"Woman shot a man. Not too bad hurt. She doctored him up, then called it in."

"Sandra said the ambulance was on its way."

"Yeah," Raymond said. "That's why I was calling you. There's a bad wreck in the interstate with multiple victims. The ambulance diverted on the way here. Bigger priority."

"Where's the victim?"

Raymond pointed to three pine trees clumped in a ragged row, the remnants of an old windbreak.

"Laying in the shade over there."

"What's he have to say?"

"Said she took his gun and shot him for no damn reason. He's Shelby Morton, thirty-four, from just over the line in Pick County."

"They're wild over in there."

"He won't be for a while."

"Can he walk?" Mick said.

"Yeah, she tagged him in the arm. A through-and-through. She cleaned the wound, put compression on it, and made him a damn sling."

"Did you arrest her?"

"No. I never arrested anybody before and didn't want to do it wrong. I locked her in the car. Been waiting on the ambulance."

"All right," Mick said. "I'll talk to her. Where's the weapon?"

Raymond opened a cargo pocket on his pants and removed a Ziploc bag containing a snub-nosed .38 revolver.

"Chief's Special," Raymond said. "First one I've seen in a long time."

"You get an ID on the shooter?"

"Said she'd talk to you and nobody else. Clammed up tighter than bark to a tree."

Mick approached the county vehicle from behind, then moved at an angle to get a clandestine peek inside. Sunlight glared off the window, preventing Mick from getting a clear glimpse until he was abreast of the driver's side. The prisoner lifted her head and Mick recognized Janice Lowe. They'd met last year during an investigation into her father's death. Janice had been a medic in Afghanistan, which had influenced Mick's decision to give her a break after a fatal shooting, a serious legal breach on his part. The situation was complex—self-defense and family vengeance—but she'd stopped short of admitting it and Mick hadn't pushed her into a confession. He'd felt snared between his legal duty as sheriff and an innately powerful adherence to the old code of the hills. Now he understood it had been a mistake. She'd shot someone else.

He opened the passenger door. Janice sat in a relaxed position as if meditating.

"Hey, Janice," he said. "What happened?"

"Will it make a difference?"

"No. But it'd be good practice to tell it before it's official."

"This ain't official?"

"Yes and no," he said. "You're not in custody. I hear you shot him with his own gun."

"Yeah, I took it from him. That deputy, is he a Kissick?"

"The oldest boy, Raymond. You know them?"

"I knew his brother when we were kids."

"Talk to me, Janice."

"He wanted to meet me. Said he knew I helped folks with their animals. Said he had a sick horse. Soon as I got here I knew it wasn't right. No fence. No pen or stall. He said the horse was hobbled over the rise. We went up that way. I kept my distance from him. I should have left. I was a damn fool."

Her voice trailed away.

"What happened next?" he said.

"He moved close and grabbed my arm. I pushed him away. Hard, I guess. He stumbled and fell. I started backing away. He got up and pulled the gun and came toward me. Maybe I should've run. But I never. I just waited till he was close, disarmed him, and shot him."

"Then what?"

"I cleaned his wound and bandaged it. I carry supplies, you know, for animals. The arm wasn't bad, nothing broke. Looked like muscle and fat, but no tendon hit.
Then I called the station. Some woman answered, then the
deputy showed up."

Mick nodded. Her story matched everything he knew
so far.

"We have to hold you for questioning," he said. "I
can't let you off."

"Yeah, I know."

"Tell me why you did this, Janice. Did it again, I mean."

She stared through the window for a few minutes,
then sighed deeply, and spoke in a calm, quiet voice as if at
a distance.

"My last year in the army," she said. "My second tour.
I was counting the time down. Two months, three weeks,
and four days, then I was done. I was at a field unit. Two
guys were waiting on me one night. Soldiers I knew. They
ambushed me. It was bad, Mick. Real bad. I knew what
to do and not to do. No shower. Take photos and get a
medical exam. Report it to my CO. He fucking covered
it up. Didn't file charges or move it up the line. Nothing
happened. Not a damn thing. They got away with it and I
still had to see them every day. One ignored me. The other
one always made a funny face, like he was laughing inside.
Laughing at me. That man today I shot, he had the same
look on his face. He was coming at me with a gun."

Mick nodded.

"I understand," he said. "I'm sorry."

"Now what?"

"Raymond will take you in. Do you have enough for bail?"

"I can use my pension."

"I don't know how it'll all shake out, Janice. But you can't go around shooting people anymore. You need to talk to somebody. A therapist or somebody at the VA. I did. It helped. Just getting it out of my head."

"You think it's PTSD?"

"I don't know. I'm not a doctor. But it's damn sure something. I'll be your friend, but I can't help you out this time with the law. Not again."

"Okay."

"You'll have to wait here with Raymond. An ambulance is coming, but it's late. You going to try to run?"

"No," she said. "When word gets out, all these pricks will leave me alone."

Mick left the vehicle and went to the victim lying under the tree as if resting from the day.

"Shelby Morton?" Mick said.

"Yep," the man said.

"You in pain?"

"Not bad."

"I'm Sheriff Hardin," Mick said. "Where's the horse?"

"What?"

"You told her you had a sick horse up here. Where's it at?"

Morton looked at his wounded arm, then past it to a particularly tall clump of pink clover. He made a face as if a sour taste had suddenly filled his mouth.

"Ain't no horse," he muttered.

"What was that again?"

"They ain't no got-dam horse!"

Mick nodded and told Raymond to take Janice in after the ambulance arrived. A rain crow gave its rattling cry like an old car engine struggling with ignition. He looked around for its long yellow bill. People thought the call presaged a rainstorm but Mick knew it was warning its mate that an interloper was near.

Not arresting Janice last time had been a mistake. He hoped that concealing Patricia Holloway's identity as an alibi wasn't another one. Or not telling Peggy about the infidelity of her new husband. He was weary of keeping secrets, of making decisions to benefit others, of ignoring his own needs. Mick wondered if his innate urge to help women had led to the downfall of his marriage. Compromise satisfied nobody. He couldn't simultaneously protect people and give them what they wanted.

It occurred to him that he no longer knew what he wanted. He didn't want to be divorced or work as a sheriff or live in his sister's house. He missed the simplicity of military life—here's your weapon, there's your enemy. Sleep, eat, follow orders. The complex and overlapping freedoms of civilian life had rendered him confused and prone to grotesque error. He could re-enlist. He could flee the hills once more. With no kids, no marriage, and no purpose, he could end his life. He didn't want to die, but he wanted to stop the suffering that he was only just now acknowledging. He wondered how long it had been there, lurking inside him. Perhaps it had driven Peggy away.

Following the code of the hills had doubled back on him, on Janice, and on the new victim as well. It was Mick's fault. The code was a burden, a terrible weight like a leather collar for a working mule. Mick was loyal to a way of behavior that was irrelevant, perhaps always had been. The hills didn't care and he cared too much. Maybe it was time to stop.

Chapter Eighteen

Mick drove back across the county to the interstate connector, searching for the trailer court that Wendell had told him about. He vaguely recalled the location of the old Long John Silver's franchise. Wendell's directions were typical of the hills, visually rooted in shared history—where things used to be. The past overlapped the present in every way, with little regard to the future. The sun would come up. The birds would sing. People would get by. Any further speculation was never worth the risk of disappointment.

One side of the road had a church and the county's first venture into a planned neighborhood more than forty years before. There were cul-de-sacs within cul-de-sacs, as if the engineers were experimenting with fractals. The other side of the four-lane connecting road held the remnants of older businesses, including Long John Silver's. Two struts held a broken sign depicting a pirate with a parrot perched on his shoulder. Much of the paint was chipped away as if the old buccaneer had caught a rare skin disease on a remote island. Mick drove past it to a strip of disintegrating blacktop. Mick stopped the truck and poked his head out the window to decipher the faded sign:

LONNIE'S MOBILE HOME PARK
THIS IS YOUR HOME TOO
LONNIE IS YOUR NEIGHBOR
ALWAYS HERE FOR YOU

Mick found the slogan oddly moving—part welcome, part sales pitch, as direct and honest as a sudden shift in season. The sign offered warmth but the rest of the place had the hard, bleak look of midwinter. Few trailers were visible. The street branched into a few lanes leading to old cement foundation pads, cracked and split and uneven. Most of the utility poles were gone—either pulled from the earth or sawn down for the wood itself. Many of the lots had been vacant long enough for weeds to grow from the gaps, as if reminding the world that people and their creations may depart but nature would always be there, a perpetual taunt of green.

Each pad had a scrap of grass as a side yard, some intended for children's play. The shell of a plastic rocking horse, its head and tail missing, lay near a crumpled swing set. One corner lot had a mini trampoline that lacked the bouncing rubber center, just an octagonal frame tipped with its legs aimed at the sky. Scraps of rotting lumber and rusty metal lay in the dirt. Mick recalled debris fields in Afghanistan near the sites where makeshift bombs had exploded. The wreckage of wreckage, with anything useful scrounged and hauled away.

Mick parked beside the rusted trough of a wheelbarrow with no tire or handles. Strolling as if lost, he entered an interlocking maze of cracked asphalt and encountered a trailer with a car out front. It was a split-level style from the early 1960s with curving edges, reminiscent of automobiles from the era, a nod toward the space age and the splendid future that never came to be.

A man stepped onto a hand-built porch. The top of a cell phone protruded from his shirt pocket. He had the inelegant build of a machine designed for work underwater—wide hips, short legs, and splayfooted. His voice was deep and mellifluous, a welcome addition to any choir.

"Looking for somebody?" he said.

"Naw, just looking," Mick said.

"Well, if you're aiming to live here, you're too late."

"I see that. What's going on?"

"You ain't with a newspaper, are you?"

"No."

"That's who we need. Or TV people. Even them influencers could help."

"Help what?" Mick said.

"We're all getting throwed out."

"Out of here? How do they do that?"

"They just tell us to leave. One month notice and we're done."

"Don't y'all own your homes?"

"Yeah, we do. Mine's paid for. We own the home but not the land it sets on. We got to pay rent on the lot."

"Can't be too bad high, can it?"

"No, it ain't. The problem is the lease for the lot. They quit renewing them. The leases. Gave us thirty days to vacate. Or they own what's on the lot. Some folks lost it all."

"What do you mean?" Mick said.

"Most of these mobile homes ain't been mobile for a long time. They're thirty, forty years old. Some older than that, like mine here. Ain't hardly no way to get them out. They fall apart if you tow them. Tires are flat. Tore up too bad to patch and they don't make that size no more."

"What about loading them on a flatbed truck?"

"Some folks tried that. The trailers buckled up and broke. All the windows popped out. The roof caved in."

"What happens if you can't leave?" Mick said.

"In thirty days you're trespassing. Anything on the lot ain't yours no more. The owner hauled all the trailers to the dump."

"Who does that? Lonnie? The owner on the sign?"

"Naw, bub. Lonnie's been dead fifteen years. His son sold it off and moved to Florida."

"Who'd he sell it to?" Mick said.

"Nobody knows," the man said. "We tried to find out, but nothing."

"Where'd the people go who lived here?"

"Anywhere they could, bub. It's been a mess for some. They's one couple had to split up. Not a one in their family had space for both of them. They're living about forty miles apart. It was mostly old folks here—widows and widowers. The rest were single moms and people like me. I grew up here. I'm what they call a holdout. There's six of us."

Mick nodded. The man shifted his weight from one leg to another but his belt didn't move. Mick understood that he had a pistol tucked into the back of his waist at the small of his back. The gun was holding his pants tightly in place.

"That gun you got," Mick said. "What are you worrying on?"

"You got one on you?"

Mick nodded.

"Then I ain't worried about nothing," the man said. "You and me, we're even. I like to keep things that way. They's been some to come in here and steal stuff. They'll take what ain't nailed down. Some pathetic people in the world, you know."

"Yeah," Mick said. "I know it. Too many. Shooting them don't help much."

"I ain't shot none yet."

"I'm glad to hear that. Let me ask you something if you don't mind."

The man's face remained still as a tree with no wind. He'd wait and wait.

"When y'all get evicted," Mick said. "Ain't that the job of the county? You know, the sheriff's department."

"That's exactly what I asked them that come around. They said it was private property and they were private security hired by the owner. Said they filed papers with the county to make it legal. One of my neighbors called the sheriff's office about it but they said the sheriff got shot and the deputy was on family leave. About what you'd expect from this county. Nothing. Not one damn bit of help. What's all this to you anyhow?"

Mick took a step back, showing respect. He spoke in a soft tone.

"The sheriff who got shot? She's my sister."

"Sorry to hear that," the man said. "How's she getting along?"

"Doing a little better, thanks."

Mick slowly moved his arms to lift his shirt and show his badge and holstered Beretta.

"I'm filling in for her but we're shorthanded. Just me and one deputy."

"They ain't been a deputy out here, either."

"He's new. Raymond Kissick."

"Fuckin' Barney's brother?"

"Yeah," Mick said. "Shifty's oldest. Raymond came back when his brothers died."

"I knowed Mason. Pretty good feller. That's a hard-luck family."

Mick nodded. That could be said of most families in the hills but the Kissicks had had a pretty bad run. Three brothers and the daddy dead.

"Anybody else I could talk to?" Mick said. "Holdouts like yourself."

"They're watching you right now. We knowed you were here the minute you came in."

"You got a sentry?"

The man tapped the phone in his pocket.

"Group text, bub. Motion detector triggered an alert. They's at least three guns on you. Are you really the sheriff?"

"For now. Raymond's got the official vehicle. I like my papaw's old truck. Do me a favor and let the group know that shooting a sheriff will draw all manner of trouble. Rocksalt cops, state police, and the FBI."

The man frowned, withdrew his phone, and painstakingly pecked out a one-fingered text. He finished and lifted his thin eyebrows to Mick in an expression of expectation.

"Another thing," Mick said. "I'm going to call the office and find out about that private security bunch that's bothering you."

"All right."

"My phone's in the truck. Tell your buddies I'm walking to it. They'll see me calling. I'll find out about the legal side of y'all getting evicted."

"You don't carry your phone? What kind of sheriff are you?"

"Not much of one, I don't reckon."

Mick turned away, maintaining as casual a manner as possible while aware that gun sights tracked his passage. He'd been in the same situation several times in the desert. The men here were similar—cornered and armed, fearful for their homes, and mistrusting of any intruder. It was important to display no fear, like approaching a strange dog or swimming in shark water. He listened carefully, scanning the periphery. As he walked, he picked out the ideal spots for concealed surveillance.

At the truck he lifted the cell phone above his head, turned in a half circle, then called Sandra. After a brief exchange, he ended the call and walked back to the trailer, where the man stood in the same position as before, immobile as a rock cliff. Mick nodded to him. The man shifted a single finger to press a button on his phone. Mick underwent a terrible memory of seeing a young boy using a cell phone to trigger an IED that had sent Mick to the hospital and killed his partner. The dread washed over him. He waited for detonation. His vision narrowed as if looking through an eighteenth-century spyglass and seeing only the man's face. It was benign, without expression, unlike the grinning ten-year-old in the desert.

Mick breathed carefully, allowing the surge of adrenaline to flow through him and into the air from his fingertips. A chickadee called. As gradual as water receding in a drain, Mick's vision expanded—the man's head, the door behind him, his shoulders, the rest of his body, and the trailer in its bleak, empty spot.

"What's your name?" Mick said.

"Thomas Oney."

"Well, Thomas, here's the way things are right now. I talked to the sheriff's station. Got a little info and am waiting on a little more. Text'll come in any minute."

"What'd you find out?"

"I'll tell all you holdouts together."

"You'll talk to me," Thomas said.

"What I'd like you to do, if you don't mind too much, is call your buddies. Put it on speaker and hold the phone toward me. I bet you got them on speed dial for a group talk."

"Why would you think something like that?"

"Because you're smart," Mick said. "And you didn't deny it. You can do what I'm asking. Or you can try to shoot me down before I get the cuffs on you."

"I ain't done a damn thing. You need to get off my property."

"I'm trying to help you. But I need your help with them other fellers. It's best if I talk to everybody at once."

Tommy's entire being took on the semblance of someone under sedation—he blinked slowly, operating his limbs as if they were weighted, and lifted his phone. He pressed two buttons with his thumb and held it with the speaker aimed away from him. Mick moved close, careful to keep his arms away from his body, palms open. Anyone behind him could see daylight between his sleeves and torso. He spoke loudly, his voice directed toward the phone.

"Y'all are fighting for your homes. I don't blame you. I'd do the same thing. But I ain't the enemy. I'm on your side. I got some info for you."

For a few seconds Mick stopped talking to let the words sink in. Thomas held the phone without wavering, his only change was a deeper frown above his eyes.

"Come on out, now," Mick said. "All y'all. One's in a rusty metal shed with a red roof. One's laying under the third trailer down on the right. They's two of you in camouflage shirts behind that dumpster with a wheel broke off."

He stopped again to let the listeners consider his request.

"You'll be safe," Mick said. "Come on and talk to me a minute."

He gestured to Thomas, who lowered the phone and checked the texts. Knowing the men would feel more comfortable, Mick kept his back turned, sparing them the visual humiliation of having their hiding places confirmed when they emerged. A boot scuff sounded to his right and the scatter of kicked gravel on the left. Mick began a slow turn until he could see four men.

The two wearing old camouflage were clearly brothers—same scrawny build, same tilt to their shoulders and pointy chins. They were nineteen or twenty, the age of cannon fodder throughout history. They held Ruger Mini-14s aimed at the sky, the mark of inexperience. Lifting a rifle to shoot was quicker than lowering it. A third man was in his forties, bearded with hair untrimmed for months. He held an AR-15 and a holstered Glock. In his youth he'd begun wearing a one-piece oval belt buckle. With weight gain, his belly had pressed it forward and down until the buckle was aimed at a ninety-degree angle to the earth.

Well back and to the side of him stood a man in his late twenties with mud on his knees, elbows, and left forearm. A pack of cigarettes was in his shirt pocket. Mick figured he was the one tucked under the trailer. His Winchester .243 rifle had a scope and butt stock on a buffer tube to cut recoil. The gun was pointed at the ground near Mick's feet. His eyes never left Mick, who understood that he was the most dangerous man of the group.

They stood in a loose semicircle around Mick. All wore jeans and work shirts. The brothers looked at each other several times as if confirming or denying secret communication. Kids, Mick thought. White kids with assault rifles, the biggest threat in the country. He hoped they wouldn't get hurt.

"My sister was sheriff," Mick said. "She got hurt and now it's me till she gets healed up."

"What happened to Johnny Boy?" the heavy man said.

"Family emergency up in Muncie. Soon as he comes back or my sister does, I'm done with all this. This kind of work ain't for me, but it's what I'm stuck with right now."

"What is it you're wanting to tell us?" Thomas said.

"First thing," Mick said. "I ain't here to run y'all off or lock you up or nothing like that. I called the station. They said the trailer park is within their rights to hire a private company to handle evictions. Personally, I don't agree, but it's legal."

The brothers kicked the ground like disappointed children. Thomas shook his head and spat while the heavy man adjusted his pants with one hand, performing the motion by rote as if he'd done it hundreds of times. His stomach moved but the tarnished belt buckle remained stationary, continuing its perpetual scrutiny of the ground below him. The man with the Winchester nodded slightly to himself. Mick understood that his words had settled something for him, an internal conflict with himself.

"Thomas," Mick said. "Where's the other man at?"

"Ain't one."

"You said there were six holdouts."

No one spoke. The brothers shifted their weight in tandem like a pair of pack animals accustomed to working together. The man with the Winchester narrowed his eyes a fraction, barely a movement, but enough for Mick to gain understanding.

"It's a woman," Mick said.

The faces of the brothers changed expressions to surprise as if Mick had performed a feat of telepathy.

"This woman," Mick said. "Where's she at?"

Again nobody spoke, and Mick realized she was related to one of the men, a loyalty they'd all maintain to the grave. Mick nodded.

"Okay," he said. "Mothers with children are gone and all the grannies, too. None of y'all are married. That leaves somebody's mother."

The dumbfounded looks on the brothers' faces confirmed Mick's speculation. The heavy man gave a quick, furtive glance toward the Winchester man.

"You said two things," Thomas said to Mick. "What's the damn other thing?"

"I know who's behind this operation. The guy who bought this place off Lonnie's boy. The one pushing you out of your homes."

Each man sharpened his attention. The Winchester man's rifle barrel lifted barely a sixteenth of an inch, but enough to indicate an overall tension that moved into his body. Mick mentally planned his response if the men attacked—shoot Winchester first, then belt buckle, and evaluate the brothers' level of threat.

"Who is it?" Thomas said.

Mick nodded to Winchester and spoke.

"I'll tell your mother who," Mick said.

Winchester lifted his rifle to Mick's chest.

"Fourth trailer down on the left," Mick said. "Blue with white trim. Two plants in the window. Somebody's taking care of them and I don't reckon it's a one of you."

Beyond the tree line a beagle howled, the sound moving away as it chased its prey, probably a rabbit. Everyone ignored it.

"We can walk there together," Mick said. "Y'all got me surrounded. But one thing to keep in mind. If you shoot me, you'll never know who's throwing y'all out."

Winchester spoke for the first time. His voice was low, a slight whisper that moved through the air like a tendril of faraway wind.

"You know my mother?" he said.

"No, I do not."

"Why do you want to talk to her?"

"Because she's strong enough to stay," Mick said. "And smart enough not to show herself."

"And if you don't talk to her?"

"I can't help you."

Winchester sidestepped to Mick's left like a cattle dog herding a cow. Mick nodded and walked forward. The other men flanked him. Mick knew Winchester was behind him but the man moved in the soundless way of a hunter tracking prey. As a group they walked the road toward the blue trailer.

Mick was applying three lessons he'd learned from war—go slow, stay focused, trust your gut. He believed Winchester had evolved from a hunter to a murderer but was controlled by a superior authority—his mother. It was a risk, all of it. His thinking, conclusion, and action. If he was right, the real risk was in the trailer, the brains behind this ragtag group of desperate men. They lived in broke-down trailers in a dying park, but it was all they had. They'd die defending it.

The clouds were high and immobile as if glued to the blue. The air was still as pond water. The trailer's door opened at their approach. Out stepped a short woman, wide in the hips and shoulders, her long hair pulled back. She held a cell phone in one hand and a .38 caliber pistol in the other. The men stopped walking. Mick continued to the bottom of the trailer steps, composed of three rows of stacked concrete blocks. Winchester stood behind him on his right, where he could shoot without hitting his mother. She had the appearance of someone who didn't care who her bullet hit.

"I'm Jimmy Hardin's boy—"

"I know who you are," she said. "I knew your mom."

"Call me Mick."

"I'm Betty Miller. What do you want?"

"I'm here for a couple of reasons, Mrs. Miller."

"Get to it."

"Yes, ma'am. What's happening here, it ain't right. It's not the fault of the contractors or the carpenters. The man behind it is the problem. Not the workers."

He waited for her to ask but she didn't and he knew she wouldn't. She'd stand there until the old wood rotted beneath her feet before she'd ask him for anything.

"It's Murvil Knox," Mick said. "He bought this land off Lonnie's son. Used what they call a shell company to do it. A way to hide the real owners. My office figured that out. Knox, he's planning on tearing all this down and putting in a big development. Stores. A movie theater with a bowling alley. Then housing. Gonna call it Rocksalt Commons."

"Uh-huh," Mrs. Miller said. "Where the common people can't afford to live."

"They ain't nothing common about you, ma'am. Or your son and the rest of this bunch. Y'all are tougher than a hickory stick. I ain't the enemy. It's Murvil Knox."

"You sure?"

"Yep, the info came straight out of Frankfort. Knox lost a bundle on coal. He was behind that mess in the Mushroom Mines."

"I heard about that," she said.

"I've had dealings with his private security firm. They're part of Blacksword. Mostly war veterans. Ain't to be messed with."

"Neither am I."

"I know that, ma'am," Mick said. "That's why I'm telling you directly. Blacksword will overwhelm your boy and these other fellers here. Ain't nothing against y'all's courage. There's just more of them. They're better armed and better trained. Knox pays them top dollar."

"You saying they're the fangs and Knox is the serpent?"

Mick nodded. He understood the implication of her question—get rid of the snake and the fangs won't matter.

"Reckon you best go, then," she said.

"I'd like to ask you one thing, if you ain't a-caring."

"All right."

"How'd you know my mother?"

"County 4-H. Long time back. She baked a good pie, but her best was Christmas decorations. She made a wreath out of dried-up eggshells and balled-up newspaper. Glued them to cardboard cut into a circle. It was spray-painted red and gold. Real pretty. Best thing any of us ever made but there wasn't no category for it in the 4-H awards. I think it disappointed her."

"A lot did," Mick said. "I thank you for your time."

She gave a nod to her son, who stepped back. Mick slowly turned, walked to his truck, and drove away.

Chapter Nineteen

Without quite realizing it, Johnny Boy had reached a plateau in his facility with French. He no longer had to imagine each word in his head, then translate it before speaking. Simple phrases came naturally. Madame Moncoso praised him and Titus said that dreaming in French was the next step.

Johnny Boy clung to his daily routines and added an hour of trying to walk without noise. Heel first was the worst. Toe first was not much better. The breakthrough was learning to press the outside of his foot slowly to the ground. At the faintest sound, he halted, then eased his weight in a slightly different way. It was simpler on the rough land of the maquis. He thought he'd improved but it was impossible to verify alone.

One night a fierce storm battered the land, the noise roaring against the thin stone shingles that overlapped on the roof. Johnny Boy lay awake until it passed. The heavy clouds obscured all light from stars and moon. In the morning the sky was still overcast, more humid but cooler, the land too wet to work. Johnny Boy decided to read. He'd finished *The Count of Monte Cristo* and started another book by Dumas that dealt with revenge—*The Corsican Brothers*—about twins who could feel each other's emotions. Once Johnny Boy got past the premise, he enjoyed the novel. It occurred to him that the story was no stranger than his own life. Maybe he was his own twin. All this was not happening to him but to his identical brother. Maybe he was the brother and had forgotten it.

In late morning he heard an automobile and stood at an angle beside the window to prevent being seen as he peered out. Sebastien's muddy Renault drove past, heading toward the village. He didn't see it return or hear the engine at night. The following day was dry enough to work, the earth soft, though heavier on the blade of the shovel. Afterward, Titus fed him, Madame Moncoso taught him, and he walked home, thinking that it was the first time he'd mentally referred to the place as home. He didn't know if that was a good sign or a bad one.

Early the next day Sebastien materialized from the maquis shortly after Johnny Boy left the house. The sudden appearance was like the land performing an illusion—the cartography of empty space had produced a human.

"Hidy," Johnny Boy said. "*Bonjour. Ça va?*"

"It goes. It always goes."

Sebastien was less guarded than during their last conversation. Johnny Boy understood that his standard air of casual repose was camouflage for his tense vigilance. Still, he seemed at greater ease now, like a man who'd taken a long sauna. A plump bird on a dead branch swelled its throat and emitted a rolling trill that managed to be both shrill and low simultaneously.

"What is that bird?" Johnny Boy said.

"Turtledove. Once there were many. Don't hurt it."

"I've never hurt any bird. What's going on?"

"It's over," Sebastien said. "There won't be any more visitors."

"Was there another?"

Sebastien kept his expressionless eyes focused on Johnny Boy's face. After a full minute, he spoke.

"Did you hear or see anyone?"

"No," Johnny Boy said.

"Titus tells me you're progressing well with French," he said.

"I can't always understand what people say. But I can get my words across. *L'accent est tres difficile.*"

"Italian is easier. Less throaty. Every syllable is pronounced."

"I've been trying to walk quietly. How did you learn it?"

"Necessity," Sebastien said. "Don't walk, let the earth move under each step."

"I don't understand."

"Listen to the dirt. Don't think."

Sebastien pivoted without sound and Johnny Boy watched him slip across the maquis, wondering if the ground had shifted beneath him. The turtledove flew away. The circling of a hawk high in the sky caught Johnny Boy's eye and when he glanced back, Sebastien was gone.

As a child in early summer, he'd experienced the surge of endless freedom when school was out. He felt similar now. Or thought he might. Insight into his own feelings had abandoned him. The Dumas book about twins held little impact because he didn't know his own emotions, let alone that of another. The inhabitants of Corsica were still mysterious and Titus never left his café. The shopkeepers treated him like an intriguing insect, not worth swatting or brushing aside. He was accepted but could have been invisible. Perhaps he was. But didn't sight depend on light reflecting off the inside of the eye, which would be invisible as well? He spent two hours pondering this with no conclusion.

He used a ridged metal file to hone the shovel and mattock, the steady rhythm its own comfort. Maintaining tools was a simple pleasure. His favorite was cutting sandpaper with scissors, the sandpaper's own function serving to sharpen the thin, tapered blades. He'd seen old men at home use a rock as a whetstone for their pocketknife, then strop it on the heel of their boot. To test the blade, they spat on their forearm and shaved a narrow strip of hair. It was surprising to witness, but a quick and easy test.

The now-familiar rattle of the Renault slid down the road as if the car was pushing sound like a plow. Sebastien opened the passenger door and waved him over. He drove in the precise manner he did everything—slow, intense, keeping constant peripheral vigilance. The road wound like a vine wrapped around a stick, ascending in tighter loops to a summit looking onto a horizon that blended seamlessly with the sea. A long series of switchbacks down the mountain gradually brought the separation of air and water into focus. The Mediterranean was dark blue like a vintage postcard. The horizon held dim humps of what Johnny Boy thought were storm clouds. They never moved and he slowly realized he was seeing the violet tops of distant islands. A narrow road, more of a stone trail with ruts, took them to a flat spot near the water. The air felt both cooler and warmer, which bamboozled Johnny Boy.

Sebastien parked and they left the car and picked their way over a dangerously rocky precipice to softer earth and a path to the water. What initially appeared to be sand was actually rounded stones the size of peas. Sebastien removed his clothes and entered the water nude, wading then swimming out until merely his head was visible. Johnny Boy had never disrobed in public. It seemed wrong, although no one was around. He watched the water for a while, getting a sense of its immensity, the power churning beneath the surface. Determined to inhabit his new life, he spoke French to himself—*Allons-y!*—and took off his clothes as swiftly as possible lest any hesitation cause him to change his mind.

He kept his boxers on. The tiny, hot stones moved beneath his feet, tender from years of protection. He made it to the water, which immediately cooled his skin. The horizon shimmered from rising mist and he lost track of where the sky began. He licked his palm, delighted that the taste was indeed salty as he'd read in books. Moving deeper scared him as the cold rose past his thighs, then enveloped his particulars. He stood for a few minutes gazing around him, seeing light sparkling along the surface. After a deep breath he plunged forward, ducking his head beneath the water, and rose immediately, gasping as if he'd been under for minutes instead of two seconds. It wasn't so bad.

He kept himself near the shore, staying in water at waist level. Johnny Boy had never learned to swim. It wasn't a valuable skill in the hills of Kentucky. There were no municipal pools or formal instruction. Those who could swim had not been taught but simply tossed into a lake by an adult. They either took to the water or they never went into it again. Now he'd gone over his head in the Mediterranean Sea. He wondered how that differed from an ocean. Was a sea smaller, larger, or the same? There were seven seas but did that include the oceans?

Sebastien appeared behind him, another of his private stunts of teleportation. He wore his unlaced boots and pants, his shirt draped over a shoulder. He stood unmoving as if fixed in place. Johnny Boy's mood was as buoyant as his body had felt in the water. He remained silent to preserve the sensation and prevent any of his joy from slipping away.

They drove to a small restaurant built into a rock cliff. The tools of cooking hung from nails on a weathered board—the biggest cleaver Johnny Boy had ever seen, a knife like a short sword, an immense pot, and strange items he didn't recognize. They ate strips of pork, drank water, then strong coffee. Neither man spoke. Sebastien paid and drove back to their little houses on the side of the rocky hill. As the water dried on Johnny Boy's skin, he felt as though a patina of salt covered his body.

He rested all afternoon, for the first time aware that he could get through things, could endure into the unknown future.

Chapter Twenty

On his way into town, Mick radioed Sandra and asked about the shooting at the construction site.

"Still waiting on the ambulance," Sandra said. "Ray-Ray says the victim is doing okay. Shelby Morton. He wants to drive himself home. If he gets his pistol back, he won't press charges. Morton will claim it was an accident. Ray-Ray thinks he's embarrassed and doesn't want people to know a woman took his gun away and shot him."

Mick's phone flashed from an incoming call.

"Keep me posted," he said. "Tell Raymond to cancel the ambulance and take Morton home."

He ended the radio call and picked up his phone. There was no one there. He didn't know the number but the area code was 313—Detroit. It vibrated in his palm with another call from the same number. The voice was familiar but undercut with anxiety.

"Mick, that you?"

"Yeah, who's this?"

"Vernon. You got to get here. This psycho bitch—"

His words were cut off by a grunt of pain. Another voice came on the line and Mick recognized the tone and accent. Originally from the UK, Nikki spoke seven languages fluently, which had softened her native inflections.

"Hullo, Mick. Lovely cottage."

"Nikki," he said. "You're here?"

"Not my idea, but yes, very much here. I need to see you. Didn't know you had guests. Hardly your style, is it?"

"Temporary."

"Isn't everything?" she said. "How soon can you get here?"

"Forty-five minutes. I'm on the other side of the county and it's all back roads. Let me talk to Vernon."

"Putting on speaker."

A few seconds passed during which Mick could hear movement and Nikki's voice but not her words. Then she spoke into the phone, the sound tinny and full of echo from the speaker mode.

"Here's your little mate. Cheers."

"Vernon," Mick said. "Do whatever she says and don't mess with her. I'm on my way."

"Okay," Vernon said.

The phone clicked as Nikki switched it back to private.

"What are you up to?" Mick said.

"I'll fill you in."

The call ended. Mick pulled to the side of the road, parking on less a shoulder and more a narrow collarbone of weedy dirt. There was no ditch but a natural rain gully. He put the truck in neutral and ran though the conversation. Nikki had rarely been in the US, let alone his grandfather's cabin in the hills. She'd used Vernon's phone, not her own. Either to conceal her whereabouts electronically, or more likely to demonstrate her location to Mick. It was unexpected, all of it, but every previous interaction with Nikki had been unpredictable.

He drove slowly to give himself time to think. Nikki was one of the smartest people he'd ever met. She could have been a high-ranking politician, the CEO of a Fortune 500 company, or a movie star. Instead she'd been recruited into MI6 and become a deep-cover spy. Her facility with languages had caught their attention along with a natural ability to fit into any situation. She could focus her unwavering attention in a fashion that made people feel as if they had a special bond. A small woman, lithe and wiry, she appeared to pose no threat, although Mick knew that was false. After MI6 training, she'd completed weapons instruction with the SAS along with lessons in tactics, strategy, and counterterrorism. Improbably enough, Mick had met her in Israel. They were part of a special course with Mossad for elite members of various international forces. The training focused on the unique skill of accurately shooting while in motion—running, or riding a motorcycle, jet ski, or horse.

Eight people began but by the end of the three-week ses-
sion, there were only four members left, including Nikki
and Mick. The rest had washed out from stress, physical
injury, or simply being too reckless.

They had come close to a sexual relationship, as close
as Mick would allow himself as a married man. A powerful attraction existed on both their parts but it wasn't worth
the potential damage to his marriage. Now Peggy had a
new husband and Nikki was in his grandfather's cabin. Life
bamboozled him at every turn.

The truck startled a sparrow, which streaked across the
road, flying low and fast, vanishing into the heavy boughs
of an oak. He recalled a sparrow that had bounced off the
window of the house in town he'd shared with his wife.
He'd gone outside and squatted beside the bird. Nothing
was broken. It was intact, merely stunned. Mick cradled the
sparrow in his hand until the bird calmed itself. Then he
placed the bird in Peggy's cupped palms. He never forgot
her expression of sheer delight at holding a bird that gathered itself in her hands and flew away. She began to weep
from joy. A few years later Peggy flew away herself.

Now his loneliness was like ancient ice—hard, cold,
impossible to grasp or chip. It would always exist, would
never melt. He couldn't let it lock him in, but he didn't
know how to halt the progression. Thinking about Nikki
in an intimate way was not the solution, but it would be
good to see her. Still, why was she here? The last he'd
heard, her career had shifted abruptly after a WikiLeaks

data dump revealed her true name, her photograph, and most of her clandestine postings. She'd returned to England chased by assassins.

He stopped at a gas station with a small diner in the back. After topping his tank, he went inside and ordered four meals of ribs, green beans, mashed potatoes with gravy, cornbread, and peach cobbler. He carried the Styrofoam containers up front, bought a case of bottled water and several bars of candy. The woman running the cash register asked about his sister.

"Getting better," Mick said. "Thanks. She'll be back on the job soon."

"Good. Linda's a role model for my daughters. They both look up to her."

"That must mean they haven't met her," he said.

Mick smiled to let the woman know it was a joke. She laughed and spoke.

"They love that she carries a gun and handcuffs. Like on TV."

"It's a tough job," Mick said. "Hope your daughters know that, too."

"What they know is their momma works forty-five hours a week standing on her feet and mostly talking to lunkheads. I'm glad you ain't one."

"Yes, ma'am."

Mick nodded and left, wondering if the lunkhead reference was a compliment, a means of flirting that he'd overlooked in the moment. He'd never know and it didn't matter. He'd long ago accepted that when it came to women, he was utterly incapable of reading the signs of their romantic interest. They had to be aggressive, like Nikki had been in Israel.

He carefully loaded the truck and drove along the edge of town. Long slants of light brightened the eastern slopes as the sun began its descent, dousing the opposite hills in darkness. Walnut, hickory, and oak grew thick on the western side, thriving in the shaded land, along with ferns, mushrooms, and ginseng. He felt a pang of yearning to walk the hills instead of constantly driving through them. It was like living on a beloved beach and never going into the water.

He made three turns onto smaller roads, relaxing into the contentment of knowing the terrain. The land didn't get old, the trees just grew. He'd driven this route hundreds of times, perhaps thousands, and never wearied of the dappled light through the foliage, the center stripe painted once during an election year, now faded to a faint imprint in places, completely gone where it caught the most sun. He knew the tight curves, the straight stretches, and the spot where rain clogged a culvert and spilled debris into the road.

Amidst the thick green of a narrow side road was a vehicle and Mick slowed. It was a big four-door rig, some kind of SUV, mostly obscured by the brush, parked at a slight angle. He instinctively checked the license plate, which was in too much shadow to see.

At the foot of the hill that led up to the cabin, he stopped and studied the dirt lane for fresh tire tracks. There were plenty, which meant nothing since it was an active construction site. He drove up the hill and out the ridge. His grandfather's cabin came into view. Sitting in front was an obvious rental car that he figured Nikki had rented at the airport. He parked, honked the horn, and left the truck, pressing his palm to the hood of the rental car. It still held a little engine warmth.

He climbed the new steps, opened the door, and went in. Nikki sat on the floor, leaning against a wall. Beside her was a bottle of water, two Glocks, a .45 caliber Kimber handgun, and four phones. Across the room were Vernon and Cro, their hands fastened behind them, their ankles held by plastic zip ties. A trickle of dried blood ran down Vernon's face from his cheekbone. Cro appeared unharmed but angry.

"Hi, Nikki," Mick said.

"You need furniture," she said. "A woman's touch."

"I don't live here. I see you met Vernon and Cro."

"You know her?" Vernon said. "She's fucking crazy, man."

Nikki shook her head and chuckled.

"They're unexpected guests," Mick said. "So are you, Nikki. What's going on? Why are you here?"

"Long story. But not here, not in front of them."

Mick nodded.

"Hey, Mick," Vernon said. "How about letting us take a piss. I was fixing to when she showed up. I'm about to bust."

"You're her prisoners, not mine."

"It's your fucking house, man!"

"Hang on, Vernon."

He offered a hand to Nikki, who ignored it. She was on her feet with a surprising swiftness, as if a spring had catapulted her from the floor.

"I forgot about that trick," Mick said.

Nikki grinned as she gathered the guns and phones. They stepped outside and circled the house for a scrap of stray sunlight and privacy. The woods were close, a thick wall of green rustling in the breeze. A chickadee gave its cheerful cry.

"What happened in there?" Mick said.

"I disarmed them, then disabled them. Are they your security? You need better."

"No, they're gangsters from Detroit. Hiding out here till whatever trouble they got into blows over."

"What kind of trouble?"

"The kind you run from and they send people after you. Something you know a little about, right?"

"That kind of thing never blows over," she said.

"What are you doing these days?"

"I'm still with Six."

"In the field?" Mick said.

"No, that's done. Special counsel to the assistant of Intel's third desk. Mainly I provide insight and give advice. Sometimes they listen. Officially, I'm a civil servant."

Mick nodded, understanding that she'd burrowed deeper into the secret world but from a different direction.

"Whatever Six wants," he said. "I'm not interested."

"Righty," she said. "You're the high sheriff now. You're running the worst safe house in history and driving an antique truck. You couldn't possibly want for more."

She glanced around.

"Pretty place, though. Except for your tenants."

"Are you in trouble?" he said.

"No, I'm not here for me."

"Who, then?"

"Sebastien."

He wondered if she knew about Johnny Boy, if that's why she was here. No, he thought, unrelated. If she'd come all this way for Sebastien, it was important.

"Last I knew," he said, "Sebastien worked for your bunch."

"He did a few jobs," she said. "Freelance. The sort Six didn't want a part of. Deniability. All that. Then he quit."

"Thought you couldn't quit Six."

"You can't, technically. But he gave up his British citizenship. Probably to avoid Six. Then he scarpered to Corsica. You've been there?"

Mick kept silent.

"That's a yes," she said. "There's a message for him."

"From Six?"

"It came through Six but I don't know its origin."

"Nothing you've said so far explains why you're at my house, let alone manhandling guests."

"The message to Sebastien has to be delivered verbally, in person, by someone he trusts. That rules out everybody except you and me. It was decreed on high that I would give him the message. However, it was also decreed that Corsica was unsafe for me. Too close to Tunisia. Threats emanating, etcetera. Six wanted a middleman."

"Why?"

"To protect the message. The plan was to let Sebastien know I needed to see him personally. In mainland France or across the sea in Italy. His choice of place to meet, repeating window, fallbacks, all of it. I'd meet him for one minute. Done."

Mick nodded. He could see where this was going but didn't yet understand why she was coming to him. It was more like a briefing than a conversation.

"That didn't work out," he said.

"Not in the least. We sent people to contact Sebastien. Experienced field agents. The first two posed as Swiss tourists, a couple. Sebastien drew them into a booby trap and they came home wounded. Not terribly, but enough to send a warning. Then Six sent one of their top men. Standout in every way. Smart, patient, expert in all weapons and hand-to-hand, spoke French with a Corsican accent. He arrives and they lose contact with him. Four days later he turns up in Sardinia. Unhurt. But absolutely no memory of how he got there. Assumption is he was drugged, possibly interrogated. This puts Six in a right pickle. They won't send another agent. But they won't let it go. They can't use local police because Sebastien is a French citizen. All this is why I'm here."

Mick nodded, thinking it through. Sebastien was the best he'd ever known and her story proved it once again. She smiled with stunning charisma.

"And for the record," she said, "I didn't 'manhandle' those plonkers inside. I slapped them about. Lightly. Now, will you do it? Will you go to Corsica and give Sebastien the message?"

"So I'm clear on this," Mick said. "If Sebastien sees a face he knows, he'll approach. That's you or me but you can't go. What about someone else? From his old unit?"

"Dead or MIA. All his close mates. Army. SAS. The Legion. There's just you. He'll talk to you. Deliver the message, then come to London and visit me."

"You've got my future planned out."

"You can't hide behind your marriage now."

"I wasn't hiding, Nikki. I loved my wife. I told you that back then."

"Your loyalty is duly noted. Admirable, respectable, etcetera. But you're available now. Unencumbered by your former fidelity."

"What's the message?"

"Does it matter?"

"When it comes to Six, yes."

"All right," she said. "But it's under strictest . . ."

Mick nodded. She lowered her voice and spoke.

"Snip, Snapp, Snurr. Red, red. Three."

"What's it mean?"

"Don't know," she said. "Snip, Snapp, Snurr are the names of male triplets from a Swedish kids' book in the 1920s. Published in England in the thirties. Seven books in the series. Analysts came up with nothing. Presumably it's code that Sebastien will know."

"Let me think about it, Nikki. Right now I've got to deal with these guys inside. My deputy's transporting a prisoner. And I'm in the middle of a murder investigation. I brought food. We can have lunch."

"Good," she said. "I missed me brekkie."

They walked around the house and inside. Mick opened a pocketknife and cut the plastic zip ties to free Vernon and Cro. They both rubbed their wrists and ankles, wincing as the blood flow returned. Vernon leaned against the wall for support. He was wearing large gym shoes, fashionable and expensive but no protection from being bound, which cut off circulation to his feet. He stretched his limbs, then glanced at the door.

"Need to drain your radiator?" Mick said.

Cro frowned. Mick gestured to the front of his pants.

"Gotta go?" Mick said.

"I do," Vernon said.

He took a hesitant step, wavered on his feet, still unsteady from the zip ties. He leaned against the wall and shook his head.

"Cro," Mick said, "you first."

"No funny business," Nikki said.

Mick followed Cro to the door and watched him walk across the patchy yard. His gait was stiff but his limbs loosened within a few steps. Halfway across the grass he stopped and looked about as if seeking the best place to go. Two rifle shots came in quick succession, the sound overlapping. A pink mist puffed from Cro's head and he dropped immediately. A third shot jerked his body.

Mick drew his Beretta and peered through the doorway. He saw nothing.

"Cover me," he said. "Shots came from the east."

Nikki moved beside him with the Kimber .45.

"On three," Mick said.

He counted aloud, then moved toward Cro in a combat run, torso curved in a semi-crouch, pistol in front of him. He heard Nikki firing into the tree line. Mick slowed as he came beside Cro, who was clearly dead, then kept going into the safety of the woods. He circled through the trees until he was near the rear of the cabin. Nikki had stopped shooting and there was no answering counterfire. He rushed across the narrow backyard of dirt and rock and burst through the back door.

Nikki crouched at the edge of the front door, her pistol aimed at the eastern tree line. Vernon lay on the floor.

"Anyone visible?"

"Nothing," she said.

"Is Vernon hit?"

"No, just scared."

"Give him a gun," Mick said.

She deftly slid one of the Glocks across the raw subflooring.

"Vernon," Mick said, "take that and go to the other wall. Stay away from the window."

"Cro?" Vernon said.

"Dead. Head and throat. The chest was insurance."

"Marksman," Nikki said. "He didn't shoot at you and me, only that guy. What the fecking hell is this?"

"My guess," Mick said, "they're after Vernon and Cro. They used that cell phone call you made to triangulate position. I saw a vehicle when I came up the road."

Mick stayed low and moved to the eastern window. He peered outside at an angle to protect his face and body. There was nothing, no sudden motion, flash of light on metal, or the reflection of a gunsight. The attackers hadn't fired at him, which could mean they were waiting for Vernon and Cro or were surprised by Nikki's counterfire. They'd regroup and come closer.

He stepped to a safe spot against the wall, opened his phone, and called Raymond, who picked up immediately.

"Papaw's cabin," Mick said. "Under fire. Need reinforcements and ordnance. Now."

"Ooo-rah."

Mick ended the call.

"My deputy," he said to Nikki. "Marine. Reliable and experienced."

"More the merrier," Nikki said. "Is Vernon any good?"

"I don't know," Mick said. "Vernon, you any good?"

"I can shoot," Vernon said. "I been shot at. But in the street, not a damn log cabin in the woods."

"Why did Charley send you down here? Who're you hiding from?"

"New guys were muscling in," Vernon said. "Robbing our crews. Charley had a drop house for money and he knew they'd come for it. Me, Cro, and another guy named Louie the Lock were waiting in there. We killed five of theirs. Louie got killed. One guy seen our faces and got away. Next thing you know, me and Cro are getting shot at on the street."

"Who were they?"

"We thought they were Russian but Charley said they were a mix. Not just Russian, I mean. Mostly Bella guys."

"Belarus?" Nikki said.

She opened the door a few inches wider while stepping back and scanning the woods, holding the pistol near her face. Her head, hands, eyes, and gun all moved as one unit.

"Nikki," he said. "Thoughts?"

"We need more intel."

"I'll do a rough recon," Mick said. "Numbers mainly. We know they'll come uphill from the blacktop. They don't know the terrain enough to encircle us."

"Yeah," Vernon said. "We were good till she used my phone to call you."

"Right now Nikki is protecting you," Mick said.

"I didn't need it till she got here," Vernon said.

"He's got a point," she said. "Should we give him up? Let his Bella boys have him?"

"Nothing to gain," Mick said. "They don't have anything we want."

"Righty," she said. "But we wouldn't have to listen to him."

Mick kept the grim amusement off his face as he turned to Vernon.

"For now we're stuck with each other," Mick said. "So quit blaming her. You can do that later. Till then it's all our mess, hear me? You watch the woods out that window. You see anything, you tell Nikki. Got it?"

Vernon nodded with the reluctance of a third grader being told to pick up his toys.

"She'll do the same," Mick said. "I'll go in and out through the back. It's a steep gully there. They won't come that way. Any sound you hear from that direction will be me. So don't shoot."

Mick left the cabin, eased past the drop-off, and pushed through forsythia and horseweed. He'd walked these woods thousands of times. He knew the trees, the folded furrows of land, the cascading light through the overhead limbs. The rabbits, squirrels, and deer were all descendants of animals he'd known as a child. The presence of the trees draped him like a favorite blanket. He'd always felt as if the woods recognized him, welcomed his arrival. Now he wanted to protect the woods from the terrible incursion of armed strangers. He went slowly down the hill parallel to the road, out of sight, ten feet into the foliage. As his grandfather had taught him, Mick was moving with the woods. He ducked low branches before seeing them. He heard the rattle of a squirrel in dead leaves. He was like a blind man who'd lived for decades alone in the same house, knowing the faintest sound, the location of furniture.

A breeze drifted among the boughs of maple as if determined to carry scent to him. He became immobile and inhaled. Aftershave. He moved more slowly than before, without sound, and another smell arrived—a cigarette. He heard the crack of a stick beneath a solid weight. He squatted and moved his vision left and right, not seeking but seeing, letting his peripheral perception kick in. Two sets of human legs. Another pair behind them. A three-man team. The legs were clad in loose camouflage but Mick had learned long ago how to spot it. The woods camo was only effective with people who didn't know the woods.

He retreated six feet straight back and continued down the hill, following the road. The enemy would be in groups to cover both sides of the road but staggered apart to avoid catching each other in the crossfire. The earth softened at the bottom of the hill, thick with topsoil. He circled through the heavier woods to the area where he'd seen the vehicle with Michigan plates, a black Suburban, its windows tinted. Beside it was a second Suburban the same size and color. Mick thought about what that meant, then moved into better position for viewing. A driver sat in the front seat with a comms unit attached to his head. On the other side, facing the hill, were two men armed with AR-15 rifles, holstered sidearms, and extra clips. They were prepared for assault, then close-quarters combat. "The men were short and wide, their facial features flat as if drawn on a skillet."

Mick stepped away, going deeper into the woods, where he could move faster without concern for sound. He needed to climb the hill quickly. Halfway up the hill he heard a car engine on the road to his cabin. It was louder as it accelerated on the last sharp turn that rose to the ridge. Mick figured it was one of the Suburbans mounting an attack but it was the county vehicle. Raymond had gotten there sooner than expected and had parked snugly next to the house. From the woods Mick saw him crouching at the front of the SUV armed with a SCAR 16S. Nikki stood at the corner of the cabin, watching the tree line, prepared to lay down counterfire if Raymond came under attack. Vernon stood just inside the door lifting a heavy go-bag up the steps to the porch. He backstepped into the cabin and Linda stepped outside and took the next bag.

Mick pulled farther back into the woods, looped around the cabin, and came in through the rear entry. Nikki spun with the Kimber leveled at his chest.

"It's me," Mick said.

Without changing expression, she returned to her position as Vernon brought in another bag. A few seconds later Raymond backstepped into the house and closed the door.

"Where the fuck have you been?" Linda said.

"Recon," Mick said. "What are you doing here?"

"She was at the house," Raymond said. "I went there for ordnance. Couldn't stop her and didn't want to waste time arguing."

Mick nodded. Linda couldn't match Raymond in a physical scuffle, but Mick knew there was no sense in resisting her will.

"Where'd you get the SCAR?" he said.

Raymond shrugged. A sound came from the bedroom and Mick turned, dropping into a crouched stance. Nobody else moved, which puzzled him until Janice appeared in the doorway.

"Hey, Mick," she said.

Mick lowered his weapon and looked at Raymond.

"You brought the prisoner?" he said.

"First, she wasn't a prisoner because the victim didn't press charges. Second, she was in the car when you called me. Third, she was an army medic. We might need her."

"Who's out there?" Nikki said.

"Three-man teams," Mick said. "They're along the road with a base at the bottom of the hill. Some have comms. Two Suburbans that can hold six, so possibly twelve enemy total."

Linda frowned, looking back and forth between Nikki and Mick.

"You two know each other?" she said.

Nobody answered. Janice squatted beside a small canvas bag and made piles of medical supplies on the floor.

"Makeshift dressings for each of y'all," she said. "I keep them in the car for animals. Any serious wound, come to me for stitching. Till then, put pressure on it. If you need help, holler out 'Medic.' I'm Janice but 'Medic' is better."

"I don't need them," Raymond said. "I got plenty for me and Mick."

Janice redistributed the piles and passed them around.

"Mick," Linda said, "who are these people?"

"Guests." He gestured to Vernon. "The ones outside are after him. Nikki, any ideas? You were in operations."

"Espionage and intel," she said. "Not combat ops."

"Raymond?" Mick said.

"They'll come at night when we can't see their approach. Flashbang grenades and smoke. Holed up in here, we're sitting ducks. Our best bet is to fight on our terms. Not theirs. Do the unexpected."

"We could retreat," Mick said. "Nobody has a stake in this."

"There's a man lying dead out there," Linda said. "In my county. That makes it my fight."

"Janice," Mick said. "Leave or stay?"

"I go where I'm needed," she said. "Right now y'all need me."

"Nikki," he said.

"I'm a ghost. I'm not here. I was never here."

Mick nodded and looked at each person, holding a stare. Nobody reacted but Nikki, who dropped her head in a nearly imperceptible nod of assent, then returned to her surveillance. The outside air would soon darken.

Chapter Twenty-One

Mick and Raymond slipped out the back of the cabin, skirted the edge of the drop-off, and entered the woods. Mick opened the trunk of Vernon's car, withdrew jumper cables, and tossed them in the passenger seat. He siphoned gasoline from the tank into three empty pop bottles left by the construction crew and stuffed a wad of cotton T-shirt into the narrow mouth of each bottle.

Mick sat for a minute, running through the steps of what passed for his crude plan. He needed Nikki and Linda in place quickly without the Belarussians knowing of their existence. The car diversion was the best he could come up with. It was also the kind of dumb trick that the Belarussians would think backwoods people might try. The only risk was to himself, so he'd embrace uncertainty and see what happened. Meticulous plans were for heists, acts of terror, and fancy parties. The chaos of combat required a loose flexibility, and his band of misfits had that in spades.

Mick drove the car out of the woods to the top of
the ridge, making sure he was not in sight of the tree line
where the enemy had been. Raymond crouched on the
far side of the car, watching the woods. Mick got out and
looped the jumper cables through the steering wheel and
around the driver's seat. He wedged two of the pop bottles
into the floorboards beside the brake pedal. The third one
went in a cupholder by the open passenger window. He put
the transmission in neutral and tapped twice on the hood
to get Raymond's attention. They pushed the car ten feet
until it reached the steeper section, where it began to coast
downhill.

Raymond stepped into the woods. Mick trotted beside
the open window of the rolling car. He picked up the Molo-
tov cocktail in the cupholder, lit it, hurled it to the floorboards, and dropped to the ground. The car continued to
coast downhill. The pop bottle exploded, sending orange
flames throughout the interior. A larger explosion occurred
as the other two bottles ignited. From the safety of the
ground, Mick saw black smoke rising into the sky and heard
semiautomatic weapon fire. Mick rose to his feet. The car
had plunged off the ridge and struck an oak. The interior
was burning fiercely with flames licking out the windows,
releasing the smell of vinyl. Unlike the dry forests in the
west, Kentucky was damp and humid, making it difficult
for fire to spread. Mick doubted if anyone would bother to
call the fire department.

He and Raymond retreated deeper into the woods away from the burning car. A gully ran to the holler and they stepped into it, able to move faster on their descent with less concern about noise. The gully tightened and they left it for a short ridge that ended at a steep slope. Mick knew the spot well from childhood. He turned his body sideways and half-skidded down the hill, his body tipped back, using saplings to hold his balance and slow his progress. At the foot of the hill, he waited for Raymond. They made a wide, looping arc through the woods in order to recon the Suburbans. The big cars were in the same place as before. The first one was empty but a single sentry stood on the other side of the second Suburban. He had a SIG Sauer MPX slung over his shoulder, a bandolier of clips, and a sidearm. A communication bud was lodged in his ear. Mick squatted behind the fender of the big car. Going under or over the car would make too much noise. Moving around either end, the front or back, would give the sentry time to respond.

Raymond held a rock in one open palm. He pointed to the front of the Suburban, made a throwing gesture, then indicated that he'd circle the rear of the car. Mick nodded and took the rock. He waited until Raymond was in place at the back of the Suburban, then tossed the rock at a tree near the front bumper. The sentry immediately turned that direction and stepped forward. Mick heard a slight gasp and stood quickly. Raymond had slipped a garotte over the sentry's neck from behind. In a swift motion, Raymond crossed his wrists behind the man's neck, bent his knees, and pivoted on his heels. He and the sentry stood back-to-back. Raymond leaned forward from the waist, lifting the man onto his back, held by the wire around his neck. The sentry's own weight began to strangle him. The man slowly stopped flailing, his limbs going slack. Raymond squatted and stepped forward, lifting his arms and uncrossing his wrists. He eased the sentry to the earth. Satisfied that he was dead, Raymond pulled the man's earbud free, listened to it, and passed it to Mick, who heard a scrap of Slavic language. He dropped the comms device and gestured up the hill.

The plan was simple—Raymond and Mick would flank the enemy and attack from behind. They'd fire, quickly change position, fire again, and continue the pattern. They'd move away from each other in a loose arc that curved back toward the enemy's rear, giving the impression of a larger force. The Belarussians would return fire but Mick believed they'd also move up the hill along the road toward the cabin, where Nikki and Linda waited in ambush. Mick knew it wasn't a great strategy. Too many variables with too little intel and too much speculation. As Mike Tyson said, "Everybody has a plan until they get punched in the mouth."

When the burning car went past the cabin, Linda and Nikki waited ten seconds, opened the door, and ran across the yard. It wasn't far, no more than thirty yards to the tree line, but they were exposed. Linda was impressed by

Nikki's motion as if she were dancing on ice with a pistol in each hand. Linda wondered if one was backup or if Nikki could shoot either-handed as a spider.

Linda felt the weeds against her knees, then she was among the trees. She dropped to the ground and crawled behind a wide-bodied maple. Kneeling, she peered around the trunk. Nikki had posted herself between two tight cedars with both pistols aimed below the thick green branches. They had made it, hadn't drawn fire, and now their job was to wait for the enemy to pass in front of them. Nikki's initial shots would alert Janice and Vernon to shoot from the cabin. The idea was a triangulated crossfire but timing was crucial.

Linda had trained in simulated combat but had never been in a gunfight. A line of perspiration collected on her brow. Waiting made her impatient and impatience made her anxious, which produced sweat despite the cool temperature of the woods. She watched the road while keeping Nikki in her peripheral vision who seemed as still and contained as a walnut within its shell. She reminded Linda of her brother but she couldn't pinpoint how. Maybe she didn't know Mick as well as she thought. She wondered about Johnny Boy—that whole story of visiting sick family in Indiana was fishy as a stocked pond. He and Mick were up to something. As soon as she was sheriff again, she could order her brother to tell her the truth. He wouldn't but she might get a little closer to it.

Nikki had said they'd wait for absolute visual verification before shooting. "If it can be seen, it can be hit," Nikki

had said. "If it can be hit, it can be killed." Linda had nodded, thinking that it sounded like a wordy explanation for
swatting a fly. She sensed motion to her right and saw Nikki
gesturing to the road with the barrel of a pistol. Linda readied
herself, hearing the soft scuff of a boot. Six heavily armed
men moved slowly on the other side of the road, using the
tree line to hide their progress from the cabin. Linda breathed
through her mouth as slowly as possible. Shoot after Nikki
does, she told herself, don't move till then.

The last man passed by. Nikki began firing both her
pistols. Linda shot at the nearest man on the road. He staggered backward as the enemy withdrew. Bullets from their
counterfire chewed the leaves around her, snapped limbs, and
smacked into a large oak. Noise roared in her head and she
lost sight of the enemy. She moved to her left and slightly
forward. Bullets shattered the trees where she'd been. She
rolled behind an oak and reloaded. The bark scraped her
cheek as she leaned around the tree. One man was charging toward Nikki's position, shooting a Hellpup AK-47 in
short bursts. Linda fired at the man's chest. He fell. Linda
crawled to Nikki, who spun toward Linda with one gun
in her right hand. She was bleeding from her left arm and
lower torso.

"It's me," Linda said. "How bad are you hurt?"

"I'm all right. Caught the edge of a burst."

Linda pulled a thick bandage from her pocket as gunfire erupted farther away, at the cabin. Nikki shook her
head.

"No time," she said. "We need to support base. What about you?"

She gestured with her free hand at Linda's leg. Linda was surprised to see blood oozing through the torn fabric of her pants. She tugged the cloth and saw a furrow in her flesh.

"I'm all right," she said.

"Let's go."

Nikki retrieved the pistol she'd lost and stood carefully, then tested her balance and weight. She moved through the woods to the man Linda had shot in the chest. Nikki fired twice into his back. Two men lay in the road. One was immobile with only his eyes moving as he breathed in hard, short gasps. The other man's chest was drenched in blood. He groped for the weapon that was still slung over his shoulder. Nikki shot him in the throat without breaking stride, then casually shot the other man through the eye. Linda swallowed to keep from retching and followed Nikki uphill toward the cabin, where gunfire had increased from intermittent exchanges to a constant roar. Nikki dropped to the ground. Abruptly the sound ended. Linda stopped where she stood, listening for movement and hearing none, the birds having fled for safer trees. Linda wished she could. Instead, she crawled to Nikki, whose shirt sleeve was soaked with blood. Linda tried to tug the sleeve up when she heard a sound behind her. She spun, lifting her gun but knowing she was too slow. Mick stood above her, holding an M4 carbine, his eyes twitching in a

left-to-right scan. He squatted, pointed to his mouth, and
shook his head—no talking.

He used a knife to cut Nikki's sleeve. The knife vanished as quickly as it had appeared and Linda understood it
went into a sheath on his boot. Nikki's forearm was streaked
with blood and ragged skin. With remarkable gentleness, he
lifted her arm and examined it. Linda saw an entrance and
exit wound, but no protruding bones. From a cargo pocket
Mick pulled a thick battle dressing pre-treated with medication, tore open the package with his teeth, and wrapped
it around Nikki's arm to cover both wounds. The entire
process had taken less than thirty seconds, then he was gone,
moving into the woods. The tree leaves closed around his
passage as if he'd been a ghost. It was a side of her brother that
Linda had never seen—the coldly efficient battlefield soldier.

Mick heard more gunfire from the cabin and eased
among the trees, shifting his body to allow the barest touch
of leaves on his clothing. Raymond was off to his right,
coming up the steepest part of the hill. Nikki would live.
His sister's wound was little more than a deep gouge. He
couldn't wait for them. He needed to press the enemy to
prevent them from breaching the cabin. He crawled on his
elbows, then rose and ran to the edge of the tree line. Two
men approached the cabin while firing. He shot one twice.
The second enemy fled behind the cabin. Mick fired while
running. The bullets struck the nearly petrified walls, and
he dropped, rolling while shooting. He found the barest

of cover behind the low walls of the abandoned well and reloaded.

From over the hill came the terrible roar of semi-automatic fire, the Shak 12 weapons carried by the Belarussians. Mick recognized the sound of Raymond's SCAR and knew he'd engaged more than one enemy. They were very close. Linda stood inside the tree line with Nikki beside her, their guns aimed at the corner of the cabin. Mick continued downhill toward the sound of Raymond's location and saw four bodies. Raymond and a Belarussian were fighting hand-to-hand on the ground, both smeared with blood. Raymond was beneath the enemy with one leg locked behind his knee. The Belarussian had a forearm pressed against Raymond's throat, whose head was tipped as far toward his chest as possible to ensure breathing. Mick didn't have a clear shot. He moved closer, his boot skidding on the slope, kicking rocks loose that bounced against both men. Momentarily distracted, the Belarussian turned slightly to the potential threat. In a sudden motion, Raymond shifted his shoulders and plunged a knife into the man's throat. The Belarussian's arterial blood began spurting onto Raymond's face. Mick dragged the man off, pushed him down the hill, and shot him twice. Raymond's clothes were so bloody that Mick couldn't tell where he'd been hit, how badly, or what needed immediate attention.

"I got four," Raymond said. "There's two more at the cabin."

Mick turned and climbed the hill rapidly. He was at the corner of the cabin but saw no attacker. Nikki and Linda were firing toward the open front door of the cabin and he knew the enemy had gotten inside. If he charged, he'd be at risk, but it was worth the gamble to kill the man shooting at Linda. He rose from the edge of the trees and ran toward the house, firing short bursts.

Linda and Nikki halted their gunfire. He sensed movement from the front of the cabin and pivoted to see Janice holding a Glock.

"Mick!" she shouted. "Behind you."

Mick pivoted and ducked. Bullets passed through the air where he'd stood, one hitting his sleeve. Janice was cut down by a burst of automatic gunfire. He fired downhill at the shooter, running toward the man, emptying his clip. The man fell. Mick slid down the yellow dirt slope toward the prone gunman, switched to a handgun, and shot him four times. Abruptly there was silence save for Mick's own ragged breath.

Mick rose and ascended the hill. Nikki and Linda had shifted position. He couldn't see them but knew they wouldn't fire on him. He ran toward Janice, who lay where she'd dropped. Just past her behind the cabin was a Belarussian lying face down. Mick shot him twice, then bent to Janice. She'd been hit four times, one a sucking chest wound. She wouldn't live long. Her eyes blinked in recognition. She tried to talk and blood came from her mouth.

"Hold still," he said. "You'll be okay."

Her lips moved and he leaned close, tipping his ear to her mouth.

"Thank you," she whispered, and died.

He climbed the steps to the cabin. Inside, Vernon lay with part of his head and neck shot away. A Belarussian leaned against a wall. At Mick's entry he tried to move and Mick shot him twice in the chest. He checked the other rooms, which were empty, then went to the cabin door and leaned out.

"Clear," he shouted. "All clear."

Linda and Nikki emerged from the woods, both walking steadily, weapons ready. Nikki's wounded arm hung loose and Mick realized she needed a sling. He descended the hill to Raymond, who had struggled to a half-sitting position against a maple that clung to the clay dirt.

"They're all down," Mick said. "Where you hit?"

"Arm. Shoulder. Hip. Right side."

"Damage?"

"Losing blood. But no arteries. Rib might be broke. Shoulder hurts worst."

"I can bring the medical kit down here."

"Get me on my fucking feet, army dog."

Mick nodded. The anger was a good sign. Still running on adrenaline, he tugged Raymond to a standing position and began the slow climb of the hill. It was only twenty feet but seemed like miles. Raymond grunted with every step, but never spoke or moaned. At the top of the hill, Mick lay him in the grass. The surrounding woods were still silent from the disruption of battle. Raymond needed stitches but he refused, and Mick opted for make-shift butterfly bandages. Finished with him, he cleaned the bullet crease in Linda's upper thigh.

"You'll have a scar, Sis," he said.

"I don't care. It's high enough to where anybody who might see it, I can warn in advance."

"Where's Nikki? I need to check her bandage."

"Following a blood trail into the woods."

He mentally counted the enemies he knew were dead. Nine, which meant if he'd been correct and there'd been ten originally, Nikki was tracking the last man, who was wounded.

"We need to call this in," Linda said.

"Not yet," Mick said. "We wait till Nikki gets back."

"Why?"

"It's what she'd want."

Linda frowned, an expression of perplexity washing over her face like a sudden rain. Mick could see the beginning of post-combat fatigue. He felt it himself but knew how to hold it off, a skill he hoped his sister would never learn.

"You might want to sit down a minute," he said.

"Where? You don't have any fucking furniture."

Mick nodded. The cussing meant she was focused. He opened the county vehicle door and gestured.

"Here you go, Sis."

There was a slight rustle of leaves and Nikki emerged from the woods, her bad arm tight to her body, the other still holding a pistol.

"You find him?" Mick said.

"Oh, yes. We had a heart-to-heart. There were ten here for a street bounty on Cro and Vernon."

"Why send that many men after two low-level street guys?"

"They killed the boss's brother and nephew."

"What's their proof of mission success?" he said.

"Cell phone photos of the targets dead. I took his phone."

"He say anything else?"

"No. After our chin wag, he had a sudden failure to thrive."

Mick nodded, understanding that she'd killed him.

"How's your wound?" he said.

"Needs a better cleaning and a new bandage."

"Ambulance?"

"No. I need to exfil. My car, too."

Mick turned away, knowing better than to offer his arm for support. They walked around the cabin, where Linda stood guarding Raymond. They all looked at each other with survivors' silence. Mick knew the bond well and knew none of them would ever talk about it. He went in the house for plastic bottles of water and a few candy bars. Nikki sat on the ground, leaning against the big tire of the

SUV, her Kimber in her lap. Mick opened the waters and handed out provisions.

"We made it," Mick said. "But we're not done. I have to get Nikki out of here."

Raymond nodded. Linda grimaced and began to speak.

"Hang on a minute, Sis. Let me lay out a plan. First, I resign. You're the sheriff. Raymond is your deputy. You're going to have to lie to the state police and city cops. Nikki wasn't here. That's crucial. Linda, you and Raymond came up here and ran into a mess. You lived, the rest didn't."

"Vernon and that other guy," Linda said. "Who the fuck are they?"

"Career criminals from Detroit," Mick said. "Vernon's got family connections here. They came down to hide out. You got an anonymous call about trespassers at my cabin."

"What about Janice?"

"Uh, tell them she's my girlfriend. She was already here."

"This is bullshit, Mick," Linda said.

"Yes, it is. But Nikki can't be here and I have to take her and her car away."

Linda turned to face Nikki.

"Who exactly are you?" Linda said.

"I work for the British government," Nikki said.

"The government?" Linda said. "Doing what?"

"She's a spook," Raymond said. "A secret squirrel."

"What the fuck are you talking about?"

"A spy," he said.

Linda faced Nikki and spoke.

"Why are you here?"

"To see your brother," Nikki said.

Linda turned to Mick.

"Are you a spy?" she said.

"No way," Mick said. "The Feds tried to recruit me but I liked the army. Joined CID and they left me alone."

"Who's they?" Linda said. "CIA?"

"And others. But the answer is no. I'm not a spy."

"What now?" she said.

"The FBI will show up," Mick said. "Maybe Homeland. The best lie is simple and straightforward. Just repeat it a hundred times. They'll separate you and Raymond but if you both stick to your story, you'll be all right. You took down foreign gangsters. That's what the Feds will look at."

"What kind of lie?" Linda said.

"You showed up and found Cro dead. Then you came under fire. You and Raymond went into the woods and engaged. When you got back to the cabin, Vernon and Janice were down. You finished off the last of them. Nikki and me were never here."

"They'll try to trick you," Nikki said.

"Right," Mick said. "They'll say Raymond told a different story, then want you to confirm or deny it. They'll threaten you. They'll offer a deal. They'll say he turned on you, blamed everything on you. But all you have to do is keep saying the same thing—both of you. No matter what.

If you don't know something or you're unsure, just say, 'I don't recall.'"

"How do you know all this, Mick?" Linda said.

"I was trained to interrogate."

"He's one of the best," Nikki said. "My advice is listen to him. I have three brothers and know how hard that idea is. Mine are mostly arseholes. But Mick's right. At least about this."

The effort to say that much seemed to tire Nikki. Her face was white and she closed her eyes as if to rest. Linda's reaction was the opposite, a kind of second wind. She paced a quick circle, brushing her hand over the hood of the car as if cleaning dust. Mick had seen her do similar things many times, often adjusting curtains, furniture, or small objects on a surface.

"It might work," Linda said.

"It will," Raymond said. "You and me, we'll figure out exactly what to say. We're law enforcement so the interrogation will be soft."

"I need to get moving," Mick said. "Nikki, give me that dead guy's phone."

She struggled to pull it from her pocket and faltered. Mick slid it out carefully, walked across the yard, and took three photos of Cro that clearly showed his face and fatal wounds. Inside the cabin he photographed Vernon from close-up angles that confirmed his death. Mick went back outside, where Linda and Raymond were conferring by the vehicle. At the sound of Mick's footsteps, Nikki stirred, reaching for her weapon as she opened her eyes, then returned to her rest.

"Got your story straight?" Mick said.

"We found a couple of holes to fill," Linda said. "First one is the burnt-up car. Second one is how Janice got here."

Mick stared at the tree line, watching a male cardinal land on a low limb as if nothing had happened and all was well. For the bird, it was true.

"Vernon's car was that way when you got here. No way to dispute it if you blame the dead. Where's Janice's car?"

"At the field where she shot Shelby Morton," Raymond said.

"Where's he?"

"Dropped him at the hospital. Then got your SOS call."

Mick nodded. He didn't think Morton would be questioned for having accidentally shot himself. He'd keep the truth to himself to save face.

"Janice's car should be here," Mick said.

"We get her car and bring it here," Linda said.

"My truck's a problem, too," Mick said. "It can't be here if I'm not."

Linda thought for a moment, then spoke.

"We take your truck and the rental to my house," she said. "Leave your truck there, then go get Janice's car. Bring it here."

"Good idea, Sis. You're getting better at this."

"You mean misleading men? I've had a lot of practice."

Mick nodded, grinning, then turned to Raymond.

"You going to make it another hour?"

"Sure, I'm good. What about her?"

They all looked at Nikki, whose eyes fluttered open.

"I heard everything," she said. "I'll make a call. Then get to the fallback."

"You can't drive," Mick said. "Where is it?"

Nikki produced a slim phone from inside a concealed pocket in her shirt. She pressed a series of numbers and letters, waited, and pressed a few more. Less than a minute elapsed and she read the texted response aloud.

"Fleming-Mason Airport. Two hours."

"They have a fucking airport over there?" Linda said.

"One runway," Raymond said. "Small planes. Private use. It's a smart choice for exfil."

"How do you know something like that?"

"Recon," he said. "Old habit."

Mick carefully changed the bandage on Nikki's arm. The blood had begun to coagulate but she needed more care than he could offer.

"Don't let her move much," he said to Raymond.

Chapter Twenty-Two

Mick and Linda drove separately and met at her house in town. He parked the old pickup and joined her in Nikki's rental. Linda headed east and turned onto Lower Lick Fork, slowing the car while Mick looked for the dirt lane turnoff. It was the longest he'd ever known Linda to be quiet and he hoped she wasn't in pain. He suddenly realized what was bothering her and felt like a fool for not having recognized it sooner. She'd never used her service weapon before.

"Your first," he said.

"First two."

"It's okay to feel bad, Sis. You're supposed to. If you didn't, there'd be something wrong with you. They killed three people and wounded you. They'd have killed all of us. We stopped them. All of us did together. Not just you."

She stopped the car and gripped the steering wheel so hard that the fake leather cover crackled. Her voice, when it finally came, was a faint whisper.

"Was it luck?" she said.

"A little, yeah. There was more of them but we were better. We lost our weakest three. But our best—Raymond and Nikki—got shot up the most."

"You didn't get hurt at all."

"No," he said. "I was lucky today."

"You've been through this, right?"

"More times than you know."

"Janice died saving you. Why?"

"I helped her once," Mick said. "I believe she thought she owed me."

"What's Nikki's story? I mean all of it."

"She's in MI6. Cover got blown and she's back in London."

"I mean why did she come here?"

"To deliver a message to me. I have to pass it on."

"What message? To who?"

"I can't say, Sis."

"Can't or won't?"

"Both," Mick said. "Like Raymond said, she's a spy. I mean a real spy. A spy-spy. That's why she can't be here. Nobody can know it. Nobody was supposed to."

He opened the glove box. There was nothing in it but a lease in the name of Jill Hansen. He read it to her.

"Is that her real name?" Linda said.

"No, but she'll have a valid passport and US driver's license in the same name."

"Is that legal?"

"Nothing wrong with having it. But if you show it to authorities, it's a felony. Plus she shot a few people on foreign soil. You're my sister and you're in this but I can't tell you anything more. This is international incident territory. You don't want that."

"Goddamn motherfucking hell," Linda said.

Mick grinned.

"You're feeling better," he said. "Let's get Janice's car and go back to the cabin."

"One more thing," she said. "Those pictures you took of Vernon and Cro. What's that all about?"

"Proof that they're dead. There's one number on the phone. I'll text the photos and they'll leave us alone."

"Why?"

"The boss got what he wanted. The other guys here, they're just soldiers who came here for the money. They knew the score."

Mick directed Linda to the turnoff toward the area where Shelby Morton had lured Janice. She parked before the damp creek bed and he walked up the hill. At the top of the rise was Janice's car. There were no other vehicles. The keys were in the ignition and Mick followed Linda back across the county to his grandfather's cabin.

Raymond and Nikki were in the shade, leaning against Mick's truck. A few chickadees flurried through the low limbs of a linden tree.

"Raymond," Mick said, "you and Linda need to run through the story a few times to make sure you both got it."

"Think they'll go for it?" Linda said.

"Yeah," Mick said. "What's not to believe? You're the sheriff and he's a deputy. You did your jobs. Lost three people from your side. Killed ten bad guys. There's nobody to dispute your version."

He wiped his Beretta down and gave it to Linda.

"Shoot this a couple of times in the air," he said. "The bullets will match some of the bodies."

"Give me Nikki's gun," Raymond said. "They'll believe I had two."

Mick nodded and retrieved her Kimber. He cleaned it of her fingerprints, then passed it to Raymond.

"One more thing," Mick said. "When they question you, don't try to give a memorized answer every time. That's a giveaway. Means you're lying. There needs to be a few small errors of memory. Discrepancies. Not giant gaps or omissions. But natural places where you might remember something a little different."

"Like what?" she said.

"Time. Two minutes or ten minutes. When you reloaded. When you moved. Small things that nobody remembers quite right. The color of clothes."

"Okay," she said.

"Give me twenty minutes to get free of the Main Road, then call it in. State and city. Call me, too. I won't answer but your phone record will show you tried to get in touch with me."

Linda nodded. He crossed the trampled, bloody grass, searched Cro's body for a cell phone, and slipped it into his pocket. In the house, he did the same with Vernon, then Janice. The info on the phones would interfere with the story concocted for local authorities. The police might wonder where the phones were but Mick doubted they'd go through the time and expense of tracking down calls. The dead and wounded would carry the weight of the narrative.

Mick examined Nikki's wounds and redressed the worst one. He helped her into the rental car, drove off the hill to the blacktop, and headed west to state road 32. The route was short, less than an hour, and he drove carefully to prevent jostling Nikki. She was leaking blood beneath a bandage. He talked to her occasionally to ascertain that she was conscious. They passed an old covered bridge at Goddard, circled Flemingsburg, picked up county road 11, then turned onto a narrow paved lane with a sign depicting an airplane. The road bisected cultivated fields of corn and soy. Beyond them, swaying in a breeze, were the yellow tops of hay. The road ended at the airfield—one broad lane for takeoff and landing and two sheet-metal hangars. A single-prop fixed-wing airplane sat behind a repair shed.

Mick parked beside a nondescript car in front of a Quonset hut. He got out, showed his hands were free, and watched two men leave the car. Both were average height and moved in a kind of glide, similar to Nikki's walk—as

if prepared to move any direction at any time. Mick wondered if it was part of MI6 training.

One man looked at Nikki in the passenger seat, then at
Mick. He spoke in a bland tone with the flat accent of a British actor playing an American in a TV show. He sounded as
if he was from the Midwest and worked in regional sales.

"She alive?" the man asked.

"Yes. Light wounds. But she needs medical attention."

"Where's her weapon?" the man said. "A Kimber."

"Not here. Is it traceable?"

"Of course not," the second man said. He shook his
head as if communicating with someone denser than the
heavy fog of London.

"What happened?" the first man said.

"Bad timing," Mick said.

"And the people who did this?"

"Accounted for."

"Fully?"

"Forever," Mick said. "No comebacks. What now?"

"Now?" He gestured to the other man. "He takes you
where you need to go. You're done."

"And Nikki?"

"Not your concern."

The two operatives opened the car door, helped Nikki
across the cracked cement, and settled her into the plane.
The first man climbed in with her and the second man
glided back to Mick. The plane taxied along the lane, made
a wide turn, and accelerated along the rough runway. Its

nose lifted, then the wings and wheels, and Mick watched the plane become smaller as it flew east and banked north toward the river.

The MI6 man drove without speaking. Mick felt weary as he looked through the window at the rolling fields. Two ragged strips of cloud lay across half the sky like scraps of cloth. A distant tree line was marked by a fence but the rest of the land was cultivated. He thought about living on flat terrain that was open enough to see conflict coming from a distance. Maybe farmers didn't think that way. He wished he didn't.

Mick instructed the MI6 man to drop him off a quarter mile from Linda's house. He got out of the car and walked along Second Street, then up Lyons Avenue. He took a quick shower, got in his truck, and headed for Cave Run Lake, a large reservoir built before he was born. It overlapped four counties and protected many towns from flooding, although its construction had destroyed four small communities.

Most of the waterfront areas had been developed for commerce but he knew a few places where locals went for privacy, usually couples. Mick drove to his favorite, a cliff overlooking a small cove. It was isolated enough that hikers didn't wander by and had no shore area accessible for swimming or fishing. The last time he'd been here was several years ago. He lay on the truck's bench seat and went to sleep.

He awoke before dawn, disoriented at first. He lay there, until his actual whereabouts washed over him. The remnants of a dream drifted through his mind and he hurried the fragments along. Most of his dreams involved being lost in a giant house with staircases to rooms filled with more steps. Or seeing his comrades blown to pieces in front of him.

He checked his phone. As agreed, Linda had called yesterday after he left the cabin. She'd called again earlier in the morning. Her voice was fatigued and he knew by her tone that she was speaking for the benefit of someone nearby, probably law enforcement trying to put it all together. She said that there'd been trouble at the cabin and she had news about his girlfriend Janice, that he should call back when he could. There were three other calls, all from blocked numbers, which meant they came from federal agencies or Detroit criminals.

He removed the SIM card from Janice's cell phone, stomped it thoroughly, gathered the fragments, and tossed them off the cliff into the lake. He did the same with the phone itself. Next, he opened the Belarussian's phone to the photos he'd taken of Vernon and Cro. He texted them to the single number listed as a contact.

Mick destroyed the Belarussian phone and tossed the pieces into the water. He did the same with Cro's phone. Then he used Vernon's to call a private number he had for Charley Flowers. He didn't expect anyone to answer. Instead it went to an electronic voicemail greeting that sounded more British than the MI6 agents.

"This is Vernon's cousin," Mick said. "The one who owes you one. Call back."

He walked along the cliff's edge, thinking about the town that had once existed below the lake. Yale had had a railroad station, a saloon, a hotel, two sawmills, and a few mercantile stores. The sawmills shut down and the town slowly dwindled until the government flooded it for the lake. Mick's grandfather had worked on a crew digging up an old cemetery to transport the remains elsewhere. The pay was good—big money, as he put it—but he'd quit after one day. The coffins had mostly disintegrated and the job consisted of raking through bones, belt buckles, and metal buttons.

Now Papaw was dead, Yale lay beneath the water, and Mick wondered if he spent too much time contemplating the past. He was born old in a dead place. At one time Mick thought that he'd have been better off living in the 1800s than now. But if that was the case, given his personality, he'd have preferred to live in the 1700s or further back, an endless movement to the past until he was a Neanderthal wishing he were an ape.

His phone vibrated. He answered and heard a voice with a thick Detroit accent.

"Who is this and what do you want?"

"Put Charley on," Mick said.

"Ain't no Charley here."

"Yeah, and I ain't Vernon's cousin, either. Tell Charley it's the army man who knows about the chameleon. He needs the information I got. It's important and it's not good."

Mick watched a red-tailed hawk crossing the cove like a shortcut to an open field for hunting. He'd never seen one above water before. The phone rustled and Charley's strained voice came over the line.

"Are they dead?"

"Yeah," Mick said. "Both of them. They got followed here. Means you got a leak."

"I'll look into it. Who did it?"

"Your man thought Belarussians. No IDs. One lived long enough to talk. Said it was for revenge and a bounty."

"Only one lived?"

"Yeah, but not too long. I used one of their phones to send proof of mission achieved. Photos."

"Of my guys?" Charley said.

"Yep. You and me, we're square. I took your boys in. Now you owe me one."

"How's that?"

"Multiple dead, plus two wounded. Feds will be involved. State lines crossed in commission of a crime. If the Belarussians are on a watch list, Homeland will be all over it. It'll get your enemy off your back and give you space to make a truce."

"Ah," Charley said. "That's why you think I owe you."

"Plus the intel about your leak."

"All right. I owe you."

Mick ended the call. The hawk was gone and he watched a cloud scudding across the sky as if towed by a ski boat. As a child he believed clouds were solid enough to ride like a pony. He rendered Vernon's phone inoperable and threw it in the lake, then used his own phone to call his sister. She answered, using the same tone as on her message—speaking for the ears of people standing nearby. He could tell she had it on speaker.

"Where are you, Mick?" she said. "I've been trying to call."

"I'm at the lake. Sorry, Sis. Had my phone turned off. You all right?"

"No. I'm with the state police. I've got some bad news."

"I'm listening."

"It's Janice. She's dead. It happened at your cabin. I'm sorry to tell you like this. I know you were close."

"Did she kill herself?"

"No. It's a long story. I need to tell you in person. Sergeant Jackson from the KSP Critical Response Team wants to talk to you, too. The FBI is on its way from Lexington."

"What's the Feds got to do with it?"

"That's part of the story. I'm at the station."

"I'll be there in thirty," Mick said.

She ended the call. Mick had a wild urge to throw his phone in the lake, then jump in after it and swim until he was too exhausted to make it back. He could inhale the water until he sank and joined the ghosts of Yale, swimming forever in a past that no longer existed. Instead, he walked to his truck and drove to town.

Chapter Twenty-Three

Over the next three days, Mick was interviewed by state troopers from the critical incident response team, field agents from the FBI office in Lexington, and two members of Homeland Security. Then they started again, asking the same questions, looking for discrepancies. Mick stuck to his story—he had gotten romantically involved with Janice because they were both from the hills, both veterans, both alone. She was tough as nails and nice as pie. Still, they'd managed to get into a spat over a minor issue and Mick went to the lake, where he slept in his truck with his phone turned off. Janice must have gone to his house to resolve things and ran into all the trouble.

During this same time, Linda and Raymond were also interviewed. Their version of events matched each other's and gave cover for Mick. Homeland took a few sniffs, concluded that the Belarussians were not terrorists, and moved on. The FBI took over the case, viewing the investigation as a ticket to a better posting than Kentucky. Part of their approach was to celebrate Sheriff Hardin and Deputy Kissick as heroes who'd engaged deadly gangsters in a Detroit drug war that had spilled into the hills. They'd been assisted by army veteran Janice Moore, who'd selflessly rendered medical care to others before succumbing to her own wounds. All three would receive commendations from the governor.

Janice was buried in a local cemetery with military honors due to her distinguished service record. It was a small funeral, attended by Janice's sister and brother-in-law from out of the county. Mick and Linda stood beside each other. Next to them were Raymond and Juan Carlos, who had mended their argument. They were living together again. Linda had returned to her home and taken over full duties as sheriff.

After the funeral Mick accompanied Linda to the sheriff's station. Inside, Sandra very pointedly ignored him, her attitude being more Antarctic than chilly. Mick understood that it was about Janice and the lie that they were romantically involved. Sandra's emotions were another victim of the assault on the cabin. She would never know the truth, always the first casualty of war.

"Sheriff," Sandra said to Linda, "we received a call from Frankfort PD. They want you to call back ASAP. About a homicide."

"Okay, get them on the phone."

Mick followed Linda into her office. The phone rang and she listened for a minute.

"No questions," she said. "I'll look into his investments."

She listened again, thanked the caller, and hung up. She shifted her focus to Mick.

"Murvil Knox," she said. "He's dead. Killed outside his home."

"Accident?" Mick said.

"Murder," Linda said. "Three gunshot wounds from a thirty-eight caliber revolver. Body found in the yard. Looks like somebody waited for him."

"Witness statements?"

"Neighbors heard the gunshots, then a vehicle driving fast. Nobody saw the car or shooter."

"Why'd they call you?" Mick said.

"Turns out he's a top investor in a business here. He bought a trailer park and is converting it to a shopping mall."

"Lonnie's Mobile Homes?"

"And how would you know that?" Linda said.

"It came up while I was investigating those three homicides. Skeeter Martin. Oscar Cook. Ronnie Morris."

"Yeah, you cleared Peggy's husband."

"Right," Mick said. "My guess is this—one man killed all three. His mom is the brains behind it, Betty Miller. They live in that trailer park. A thirty-eight was the murder weapon for all three of my victims. I bet Knox was killed by the same weapon. I believe it belongs to the Millers."

"How would a guy living with his mom learn who the big secret investor was?"

"Might've come up in conversation," Mick said.

"Uh-huh. You saying you told him? You sent him after Knox?"

"What I'm saying, Sis, is that in the course of a homicide investigation, I suspected that the murders were connected. I interviewed people at the mobile home park. Nobody admitted anything but I think if you lean on the Millers, they'll break. The son will fold like a bobby pin and try to take all the blame to protect his mom."

From his pocket, Mick removed a plastic bag containing two cigarette butts and slid it across her desk.

"I found this behind Ajax. My hunch is they'll match the Miller boy's brand. Might be DNA there, too."

Linda sat immobile for two minutes, the longest time he'd ever seen her utterly still. Her breathing was normal and she blinked her eyes at a standard pace. She was back on the job. Finally she spoke, her voice modulated, tone low.

"They're armed and dangerous," she said. "The only way to arrest them is together. He won't risk his mom getting hurt by resisting."

Mick nodded.

"So," she said, "you'll need to surveil their trailer. Ray-Ray and I will be out of sight nearby. When you confirm they're both present, we'll move in. Make the arrests."

"Good plan," Mick said. "But two things. The mobile home park is in the city limits, which means involving Chief Logan."

"What's the second thing?"

"I can't do your surveillance. I don't work here any-more. I'm going to the airport tonight."

"Where to?"

"Errand for Nikki."

"When are you coming back?"

"I don't know," Mick said. "I'll stay gone long enough for the dust to settle on all this. I didn't make any notes or records about what I learned at the trailer park. Probably won't come up. But if it does, I'll be unavailable."

"Unavailable for what?"

"Anything, Sis. I might be gone for a while."

"Doing what?"

Mick looked at the spartan furnishings of the office. A couple of photos of Linda in a dress uniform posing stiffly with political bigwigs. Soon there would be framed com-mendations for the bloodbath at the cabin.

"I got tired of being in the army," he said. "And I didn't like being sheriff. All I ever wanted was to come home and live with Peggy. That fell apart and I thought I'd be okay in Papaw's cabin. But I'm like a curse on it, Sis. First it burnt down, now it's a crime scene. I don't want to be there anymore."

"Where will you go?"

"Not sure. Where Nikki's sending me. Then see what that leads to."

"I never understood you, Mick. I still don't."

"Me neither," he said. "Maybe I should try a Tibetan monastery. Sit still and see what unfolds. Meditate. Give up attachments."

"I'd say you're doing that last one already. You're a damn expert at it. Just don't give me up, too."

They stared at each other for a long time, simultaneously blinking damp eyes, both deeply uncomfortable with their shared emotion. Mick stood.

"I got to go," he said. "Bye, Sis."

She stood, came around her desk, and hugged him hard. He couldn't recall the last time he'd been hugged, and never by her. His impulse was to resist in every cell, but he made himself relax and hug his sister back. She released him and turned away.

He left the room and stopped beside Sandra's desk until she glanced at him.

"I'm sorry," he said. "You deserve better. I hope you find it."

He drove to his sister's house past buildings and trees that he'd seen hundreds of times. Some people drew comfort from small-town life but it was oppressive to him. Even the trees seemed stunted. He called Raymond, told him he was leaving, and asked him to take care of his pickup truck. Raymond agreed without question. They hung up and Mick called Albin to arrange for a ride to the airport.

Mick stood in his mother's kitchen, where everything had remained in the same place for forty years. The only changes were a new stove, refrigerator, and automatic dish-washer. It was clean and tidy, but soon it would reflect the disarray that Linda left behind like the wake of a boat. He carried his army duffel bag to the edge of the driveway. Albin's car came up Lyons Avenue at the pace of a child on a tricycle.

"Sit up front, Mick," Albin said. "I hate all this stuff you been through."

"Not a word, Albin," Mick said. "Not one more word. Just drive me to the departure gate. You understand? Zip it up."

Albin turned the car around, drove through town to I-64, and headed west to Lexington. Mick closed his eyes. He loved the land but he felt as if the land was done with him, that he'd betrayed it by spilling too much blood among his beloved trees. He drifted into a partial rest, jarred to alertness when Albin exited the interstate and began the slower drive to the airport. He gave Albin four hundred dollars and walked into the terminal and waited at his gate. He flew to Atlanta, upgraded to business class, then boarded an international flight to Paris. His body began relaxing at the moment of takeoff. Aside from being alone in the woods, he'd always felt most relaxed on an airplane, moving between worlds in which he did not fit. He slept most of the way across the Atlantic.

Jet lag gnawed him at the layover in Orly, where he boarded a smaller plane to Corsica. The other travelers were mostly German tourists. The French didn't often visit

Corsica, which was part of the reason Mick liked the island. Being ignored gave the inhabitants greater freedom. It was the same in the hills.

In Bastia he rented a car and drove along the cap toward the village near Sebastien's place. He carried his duffel into the café, where he ordered the day's special and a coffee. The barman pretended not to notice the conspicuousness of his newest guest. That was enough for Mick, who knew that the man would notify Sebastien that a stranger was here. He ate slowly and drank another coffee, giving the courier time to get up the road, probably a kid on a moped.

He paid his tab, thanked the man in his rough French, and drove out of town and up the hilly road. He passed a building and wondered if Johnny Boy was staying there. Mick parked at Sebastien's house, left the tiny car, and leaned against the door. Sebastien stepped around the side of the house. He was smiling as he tucked a pistol into a shoulder sling beneath a light jacket. Mick had forgotten how heavily Sebastien dressed regardless of warm weather. They stood out of arm's reach of each other, old habits of security, and waited for the other to speak.

"Nikki sent me," Mick said. "A message came through Six, but it's not from them. Had to be personal and verbal. Six sent three others who ran into problems along the way. Maybe you know about them already."

Sebastien's face gave nothing away. He was as unreadable as cursive would be to future generations.

"Message is this," Mick said. "Snip, Snapp, Snurr, Red, red, Three."

"Repeat."

"Snip, Snapp, Snurr, Red, red, Three."

Sebastien's pupils tightened slightly and a line along his left eye briefly deepened. Mick wondered what the code meant to him.

"Anything you need me to do?" Mick said.

"No."

"Care if I stay awhile?"

"Long as you want. You still remember where the munitions are stored?"

"Yes."

"There's more now," Sebastien said. "More cash, too. I added a room but the entrance is the same. Nobody knows about it but you."

"What's the barman know on Johnny Boy?"

"Just another Yank."

"Is he fit for duty?"

"Yeah. He's sorted. He talked to me about it once."

"Glad to hear it."

"I don't know what he was before, but he's good now. Gone native and half feral. Chasing around after a cat-fox."

"What's that mean?"

"He'll tell you. Why'd Nikki send you?"

"Too dangerous for her. There's still people waiting for her to surface."

"I'll need a ride."

"Sure," Mick said. "Any idea when you'll be back?"

"None. Two weeks. Maybe two months or years. Maybe never. There's a last will and testament in the munitions bunker. Solicitor's in Bastia. All the info is there."

"You'll come back," Mick said.

"It'll be a tight one."

"I should go with you."

"If it's not me alone, they'll kill us both."

"I can hide and cover you."

"I know you can, Mickey. But these blokes are good."

"Then why do it?"

"I owe a guy. This'll put us right."

Mick nodded. In addition to being the closest either had to a friend, they were professionals, which meant accepting certain terms. They looked at one another for a few seconds, then Sebastien turned away, heading toward his house. Mick went to the rental car for his duffel bag.

Sebastien's house appeared small on the outside but seemed bigger inside due to the single big room, and additions in the rear. Constructed of stone, it had exposed beams, comfortable furniture, and a large, fully equipped kitchen. Windows on all four sides gave clear views to any approach. One wall had a series of monitors from several live-feed cameras, triggered by motion anywhere on the property. A human stepped into the frame of one screen. Mick enlarged the image and recognized Johnny Boy with a few days' growth of beard.

Sebastien entered the room carrying a soft case composed of numerous zippered pouches and a long strap. He tossed a set of keys on the scuffed kitchen table.

"This place," he said. "Jean's door. And my car."

"Mail?"

"Goes to the bar in town. Owner will take care of it."

"Anything else?"

"There's a SAT phone in the bunker if you need it. Your cell will work in places. Jean can show you where to stand."

They walked outside to the rental and headed back along the winding cap road to Bastia. Between patches of trees, the Mediterranean was visible, brilliant aquamarine with streaks of pure green. Sebastien drove slowly. He exuded an attitude of calm as if out for an old-fashioned Sunday drive instead of responding to an emergency SOS.

Sebastien turned onto a dirt road that reminded Mick of home—no ditch, very narrow, weeds flaring on both sides. It faded into grassy rock at a low bluff. A faint path led to a crude dock where a surprisingly large and powerful cabin ship was moored. Sebastien parked and unloaded his gear. Mick went with him. At the head of the path, Sebastien looked at the boat, then at Mick, and shook his head.

"Just me from here," he said.

"Thanks for taking in Johnny Boy," Mick said.

Sebastien nodded, then moved down the rocky path to the dock. Mick got in the car and drove back along the road, its beauty wasted on his exhausted state. At Sebastien's house, he undressed and slept for twelve hours.

After a shower and food, he went outside and found Johnny Boy standing in the road like a granite whistle post for an old railroad. He wore the clothes of an Italian peasant despite being on a French island. His ruddy skin was darker, his shoulders broader, his forearms strong from work. His hair was long and unruly as if brushed with his fingers. He'd filled out with muscle and moved in a different way than before—looser, his limbs less tightly joined, his shoulders relaxed. His eyes were the most different. They had hardened and softened as if the wisdom of decades had swept through him in a few months.

"Hidy, Mick," Johnny Boy said. "How's Linda?"

"Docs fixed her up. No limp. How are you doing?"

"Good, I think. Sometimes I don't know. Not so many folks to compare myself against. First time I've talked American in a long time."

"Feel rusty?"

"Yeah, I learned some French."

"How's your sleep?" Mick said.

"Good now. Pretty bad for a while. But all the labor he had me doing wore my body out. Turning off my mind was the hard part."

"Always is."

"For a long time I was homesick so bad I couldn't stand it. But I'm more used to it now."

"It's a good place to heal up," Mick said.

"You know they got an animal here called a cat-fox. Three feet long. Tail like a raccoon. I seen one. Way up high on a ridge. More'n a mile up."

"I don't think a cat and a fox can mate."

"Naw, they just call it that," Johnny Boy said. "It's more like a cat than anything. But big as a fox and moves like one. They got university scientists out here studying them. You know, from the mainland and all. You want to eat lunch? Titus has got some pictures of it."

Mick nodded and they walked the road to the bar. Mick had been here barely twenty-four hours and he'd already made this same brief trip four times. It was a pleasant journey. He stopped when he glimpsed a pig.

"*Porcu nustrale*," Johnny Boy said. "They're all over the damn place."

"You ever think about going home?"

"At first that's all I thought about. Then I just tried to focus on being here. You know, what was right in front of me. But yeah, I think about the hills every night."

They ate the day's special at the bar, served by Titus, who treated Mick with an exaggerated respect. Having two rare Americans in his establishment delighted him. Titus showed Mick photos of what appeared to be a large cat with a bushy tail.

"*Ghjattu volpe*," he said. "A new species! The first new one in this century. In all the world."

"*Tout le monde*," Johnny Boy said.

A woman came in and Johnny Boy spoke to her in French, then introduced her as his *professeur de langue français.* She responded as if correcting his use of the term, shook Mick's hand, and in a formal tone said, "It is very nice to make your acquaintance."

She left and Mick reached in his pocket for his wallet but Titus waved him off.

"Not today," Titus said. "Not here. You are my guest."

"*Merci beaucoup,*" Mick said. "*Le repas était délicieux.*"

"You are welcome," Titus said.

"*À tout à l'heure,*" Johnny Boy said.

They left the café and walked back along the road silently. At Johnny Boy's house, they stopped.

"Sebastien left," Mick said. "I'll be staying at his place."

"For how long?"

"No idea. Linda's back on the job."

"Who's her deputy?"

"Raymond Kissick."

"Ray-Ray?" Johnny Boy said. "I don't believe it."

"It's true. The county's got enough budget for two deputies now. Linda needs a senior man. Someone with solid experience. Someone she trusts."

"What about you?"

"I'm tired of it. All of it. Law enforcement. Eldridge County. There's not a place for me there now."

"It's the only place I ever wanted to be."

"You can go back, Johnny Boy. If you want to."

"What about what happened and all?"

"Squared away completely. Case is closed. You're in the clear."

"Think I'm ready?"

"Sebastien thinks you are. You have to decide for yourself. But yeah, I'd say you're ready."

Johnny Boy nodded twice, then turned away and entered his small stone house. He was the same, Mick thought, but stronger. Better. At least he didn't talk so damn much.

Mick climbed to the top of the rocky crag, where he could see a clear scrap of the Mediterranean. He lay down and looked at the sky. He felt as if he could rise into the air and join the clouds drifting across the rich blue sea. He was free, truly free. Unencumbered by job, marriage, land, or family. He could do what he wanted, live anywhere. He'd given everybody a break for years and years. It was time to give himself one.

Acknowledgments

This book would not exist without the following people.
My deep and eternal gratitude.

Michael Carothers
Cindy Johnson
Jonathan Ames
Scotty Hyde
Gina Shulimson
Jon Hart
Sam Offutt
Keiko Offutt
James Offutt
Genna Offutt
James Milliner
Ivo Kamps
Randy Ryan
Tony Swofford

Manuela Gessica Montanaro
Lorca Wood
May Mantell
Sandy Dyas
Jonathan Lethem
Sebastien Bonifay
Mike Box